Anonymous

Lynton Abbott's Children

A Novel: Vol. I.

Anonymous

Lynton Abbott's Children
A Novel: Vol. I.

ISBN/EAN: 9783337051488

Printed in Europe, USA, Canada, Australia, Japan

Cover: Foto ©Andreas Hilbeck / pixelio.de

More available books at **www.hansebooks.com**

LYNTON ABBOTT'S CHILDREN.

A Novel.

IN THREE VOLUMES.

VOL. I.

London:

SAMUEL TINSLEY & CO.,

10, SOUTHAMPTON STREET, STRAND.

1879.

LYNTON ABBOTT'S CHILDREN.

CHAPTER I.

MY earliest years were spent in a quiet and happy home in Devonshire. Never a day passes but I think tenderly of the old place. My heart clings around the ivied walls and the picturesque turrets, with their surroundings of abrupt hills, of green meadows, and of patches of dark woodland, which make up the ancestral dwelling-place of my name, the home of my early days and of my young womanhood, and at this day the domain of my kin. I never have seen, and I never shall see, a place which will attach

my affections as they are held by Abbey
Castle.

My father and mother had held rule over
the Castle, with its broad lands, and the
dependent village of Apsland (probably a
corruption of Abbotsland) for fifteen years
before I was born. Six brothers had preceded me in entrance into the world ; and
very happy, no doubt, was the Squire's
lady when, at last, a daughter was laid in
her arms.

My father, however, was somewhat displeased by the intelligence that his seventh
child was a girl. He, himself, was the
eldest of ten sisterless brothers ; and singularly enough, his father also had been blessed
with a large family of sons without any in-
termingling of daughters. My father had
thus been led to expect that he also should
have ten sons to carry on his name in the
world. So fixed was this expectation in his

mind, that, soon after the birth of his first son, he drew out a list of his intended children's names, and the profession which each should follow. Those names and professions were all masculine.

The eldest was, of course, named Lynton, after the master himself, and was destined to succeed him in the estate. The second he would name James, after his eldest brother ; and the destiny of this boy was the army. The third, to be called Marshall, was to adorn the Church, following in the steps of our uncle, Dean Marshall Abbott. The fourth, Everard, was designed for the diplomatic service; the fifth, William, for medicine ; the sixth, George, being so much younger than James as not to interfere with his elder brother, was also to enter the army.

Then came the seventh on my father's list, thus :

' Henry Abbott ; to be allowed the choice,

at the age of eighteen, between the Church and physic.'

The first six children had carried out this programme in that they were all boys, and were named after their uncles and great-uncles according to the ancestral list. So my father was, doubtless, quite unprepared for the truth when my old nurse entered the library one fine spring morning, bearing upon her arm his seventh child.

'Ah!' said my father, taking the new scion of the root tenderly into his arms. 'So here is my little Henry — Mow — ow —oo,' and the other indescribable noises which people are in the habit of making over babies were duly enunciated.

'I beg pardon, sir,' said nurse, as soon as she could make herself heard ; 'it's not a boy, sir ; it's a girl.'

Nurse (who was an aged woman living in a cottage in the village on a pension when

I grew up) has often related to me the haste with which my amazed sire returned me to her arms. Indeed, if she spoke truly, I was barely saved from a tragical end similar to that of the renowned 'Humpty Dumpty.'

My father was not wont to make a display of his emotions; and after this first involuntary exhibition of disappointment, he rarely showed his regret. But that he felt it was rendered visible by two or three circumstances. He had personally superintended the arrangements for the public baptism of all my brothers, which ceremony was performed as each arrived at the age of two months. My mother waited patiently for the expression of his wishes in this case. But when two full months had elapsed, and her husband had made no sign of remembering that his youngest child had no name, she ventured to broach the subject.

'When shall baby be christened, Lynton?' she asked one evening.

'Just when you choose,' replied my father, with a 'No-business-of-mine' air.

'Shall it be next Thursday?' enquired my mother, presently.

'I tell you once more, my dear,' answered the master testily, 'that you may decide for yourself. Find the necessary people, and trouble me no more about it. Of course, I will be there, if you will let me know when it is to be.'

But fifteen years' study of her husband's character had made my mother cautious to do nothing without his assent. So by-and-by she ventured again.

'I was thinking of calling baby "Margaret," after her aunt, Lynton.'

'The child's name,' said my father, emphatically, 'has been fixed for years. It shall be called Henry, as was the seventh child of my father, and of his father before him.'

'Thus saying, he rose and left the room, to avoid remonstrance, leaving my mother aghast. However, that gentle lady seems never to have wilfully disputed against the strong will of her taciturn, proud, autocratic husband; and so the baby was christened in the name he ordered, made feminine at the font by the addition of 'etta.' From thenceforward I rejoiced in the possession of two names, to either of which I answered as readily as to the other. By my mother and by the servants I was spoken of as Miss Hetty. My father and brothers invariably called me Harry.

A little over one year after this the last of my brothers was born. His name and career were fixed, of course. He was to be called Charles, and when a man was destined to become a barrister.

There yet remained place and name for two sons; but they never came. Soon, very soon, after my father had welcomed his eighth child, he was called upon to bid a last adieu to his beloved wife.

' Be careful of my little Hetty, Lynton dear,' were among my mother's last words, as I have often been told. 'She will grow up to be a comfort in your life one day.'

Then clasping her babies to her breast, and casting a last look of love upon all her children who wept around, the gentle lady fell asleep.

' So I was deprived of my mother's care before I was old enough to know my own loss. From all that I have heard of her it was indeed a deprivation. She seems to have been singularly sweet and gentle in temperament, and to have had a wonderfully softening and brightening influence

upon my father's stern and somewhat
gloomy nature. How great her influence
must have been was shown by the change
in my father's habits upon her death. He,
who until then had been notably hospitable,
withdrew himself almost entirely from
society. He never visited his relatives,
nor invited them to visit him. To go
about the house she had adorned ; to care,
after his own peculiar fashion, for the
children she had left him; and to have no
sort of gay distraction from constantly
dwelling on her memory, seemed to be the
aims of his daily existence. He appears to
have always had a habit of thinking for
himself and of acting out his thoughts ;
of unswervingly doing as he thought fit,
and of not accommodating himself to other
people's ideas — which had been held in
check by his wife's influence. When her
gentle guidance was withdrawn, the course

of life which he pursued, though unob-
trusive, was decidedly 'eccentric,' as it is
customary to call anything strongly original.

His brothers and their wives told him
that he must have a lady housekeeper, and
a governess. My father was not in the
habit of speaking bluntly enough to *say*,
but I dare say he *thought* 'To scheme to
marry me!' He most decidedly refused to
adopt the suggestion; and possibly the per-
tinacity with which it was pressed upon him,
led him to withdraw so much as he did
from correspondence with his relatives.

He led almost a hermit's life, and the
establishment was managed upon co-opera-
tive principles. Mrs. Stillingfleet, the housekeeper, who had been my grandfather's
servant before she was my father's, and was
a staid woman of fifty now, was invested
with supreme power in the internal direction
of the house. Jane, our devoted old nurse,

had authority to care for the bodily needs
of the five boys then at home, and myself,
while my father took the posts of general
overlooker indoors, of director of the edu-
cational and bill-paying departments, and,
dismissing his steward, himself undertook the
management of his large estate. His time
was thus completely filled up, and his
establishment kept in train.

So far as the physical results of this com-
plicated scheme went, nothing was left to be
desired. Tall, strong, and robust, my young
brothers and I became. But about the
mental and moral results!—well, what do
you think they were likely to be? Could
the fragile plant of young ladyism be reared
in this bracing out-door atmosphere? Ah,
Mr. Tennyson! with all your knowledge of life
and human nature, I suspect you were mistaken
when you made your Elaine, who declared

' My brethren have been all my fellowship,'

so weak, so pliable, so very womanish ; Enid
or Guinevre might have grown up under
such conditions, but lily-white maidens grow
in drawing-rooms. If dying for love, and lying
awake all night to brood over a stranger's
dark—splendid face, and all the rest of it,
are to be desired, then such an education as
mine should not be given your girls. But
let me show the results, and leave the verdict
to my readers.

It is one day removed by rather more than
ten years from that on which my father was
first horrified by the information of my
sex. I and three brothers—Willie, George,
and Charlie—have been duly aroused from
sleep at six in the morning, and arisen
from our various beds, to assume our individual attire. Wonderful as to texture were
the garments of us all. Nurse bought the
thickest of cloth, the stoutest of winsey,
for our use ; for she said, with truth, that

' them boys—and Miss Harry, too—was for ever a-dragging, and pulling, and catching, wherever there was branch or nail to catch on, so as one pair of hands never could a-kep 'em tidy if so be as they wasn't dressed in things as could stand a little.'

But the wonders of *my* vestments did not cease with texture. I was the playmate of boys—how could I wear the ordinary clothes of a girl ? My petticoats, therefore, were made scanty and short, and beneath them frilled trousers descended to my ankles.

This sensible alteration in my costume had been made by nurse's wisdom very early in my career. When I wore the ordinary dress, the skirts were nightly found reduced to tatters, saturated with wet from dabbling in the lake, buttonless and stringless ; while my knees were barked by my frequent tumbles, and my bare arms scratched by brambles and briars into piteous condition.

Nurse silently bemoaned my fate; but she dared not venture on a remonstrance with my father, whose authority supported me in my favourite boyish pursuits; so she wisely accommodated her arrangements for my personal comfort to the exigencies of our circumstances.

Add to this, that my hair was cut short, and that it perversely would not lie straight except when parted to the side, and you will understand that there was very slight difference in the external appearance of myself and my younger brother Charlie, when he, in his all-round holland pinafore, and I ran off together, after our elder brothers, to attend to the morning wants of our numerous animal pets. The master—as even we often called our father in speaking of him—permitted all of us to keep just such animals, and as many of them, as we might choose; he only appended the condition, that they should never be neglected. To ensure this, there existed a standing order, that every morning before we received our breakfast, and every night before our supper, nurse should inquire 'Were the pets fed?' And it was also impressed upon us, that if the master discovered any animal in a dirty and unsatisfactory condition, permission to keep pets would be removed from the derelict owner.

But we inherited our father's gentleness to the helpless things dependent on us for happiness. We had a remembrance, so vague that it was almost a tradition, of our brother Marshall having transgressed this law, and of the storm of the master's wrath. But even William, my senior by three years, and five years younger than the criminal Marshall, had never known exactly what the offence had been. And the uncertainty surrounding the fact, invested it with horror, and gave to the dimly remembered figure of our elder brother—who was now studying with our uncle, the Dean, preparing for College, and for the Church—a black and terrible outline. I mention this because I cannot doubt that it influenced my feelings toward my brother Marshall all through my life ; and, also, because it is curiously illustrative of how truly ' the boy is father to the man.'

Our various pets attended to, the four of us returned to the house to breakfast ; and at nine, we proceeded together to the library, where our father awaited us.

Up to the age of fourteen, the master, who was an accomplished scholar, had taught all his boys himself. Lynton, James, and Everard, had passed out of his hands to Rugby, where the last-named still remained, and from whence the two elders had pro-ceeded to Oxford. But Marshall, who came between James and Everard, had never gone to school, but had been sent straight from his father's to his uncle's tuition ; and this fact may, perhaps, help to account for the disposition, so different from that of all the others which Marshall developed.

Willie, the eldest of those four of Lynton Abbott's children who were at home on the day I am describing, was thirteen, and would be leaving home in a few months for school. George was only eleven, and Charlie nine, with myself midway between these two.

Willie was deep in Virgil, and very skilful at discovering which word out of the third line below had to be brought up to the one under consideration ; for which I then supposed him a prodigy. After he had construed for half-an-hour, George performed various evolutions with irregular verbs, and struggled with Cæsar. Then I was called upon to develop ' amo ' and its

companion intricacies of tense. Then Charlie
produced the declensions in perfection ; and
finally we all brought composition for examination. After this came various arithmetical
and mathematical difficulties, and English
grammar and composition ; and the morning
and our studies ended together with the
only remarkable feature of the master's
teaching.

To the end that his children, when they
were grown, should go the way he desired
without absolute compulsion, my father was
used, not only to always speak to each one of
his future lot in life as a settled thing, but
to actually set lessons to each of his children
in the subject which must be the study of
the future life.

It would be comical to remember, if he
had not been so serious, how completely
my father ignored the fact of my sex. He
behaved to me always precisely as though

I had been the boy for whom he had looked, and by whose name he addressed me. You remember, perhaps, that the seventh son was to be permitted to make election for himself between the Church and medicine as professions. My Uncle Henry had chosen the latter; but he had been allowed the choice by my grandfather. No such freedom of selection was given to the elder son, Marshall; there was a family living, and whether he wished or no, he must prepare for it. But Henry—that was me—would have to make his own way, to a considerable extent, in either profession; and, therefore, might choose. Text-books of medical subjects had been placed in my way, and my taste watched, just as though I had, indeed, been my father's seventh son.

Fortunately for myself, I developed a very strong taste for medical study in all its branches. It was most intensely in-

teresting to me. For the sake of knowing,
I even gladly surmounted the difficulties
presented by the long anatomical names ;
and to study the more fascinating parts of
anatomy was to me a delight rather than
a task. Willie and I, therefore, were both
engaged upon a large book of anatomy,
and in this subject we were equals ; for
though he made no objection, and had no
downright distaste for the profession of his
father's choice, my bright sweet-tempered
brother had none of my enthusiasm in the
study.

For an hour he and I sat side by
side in one great armchair, conning over
the names of the muscles of the front of
the forearm ; and such light and easy facts,
as that 'The pronator radii teres is a two-
headed muscle. The larger head arises from
the humerus, immediately above the inner
condyle, and is also attached to the fascia of

the forearm. The other head arises from
the inner side of the coronoid process of the
ulna,' etc., etc. Meanwhile, George sat
with our father at the table, building fortifi-
cations with straws, from diagrams in a
military work. When we had mastered these
tasks, our morning's work was over.

' Harry,' said Willie to me, as we sat at
the dinner-table, ' wouldn't you like to keep
a hedgehog ?'

' No, thank you,' I replied, ' I've got all I
can do with already. But if you are going
down into Apsleigh, old fellow, you might
call and get me my pocket-knife—it's at the
blacksmith's, being riveted.'

Willie readily promised to bring it home
for me—I did not foresee the poor knife's
fate ; and he and George departed to Apsleigh immediately after dinner. Thus
Charlie and I were left alone, and our
ordinary afternoon cricket was neglected in

consequence. I secured a new book, and
went out into the park to read it.

Believe me, you unfortunate young ladies
who have no experience in the matter,
there is no more delightful place for reading
a new book than one of the higher branches
of a tree. The trees in the apple-orchard,
bending under the weight of the fruit which
the July sun was ripening, were my favourite
retreat. Choosing one of the largest and
sturdiest trunks, I deposited my book in my
pocket, and soon was comfortably arranged
upon the highest branch which would sup-
port my weight.

I suppose I had sat there about an hour,
when I glanced up from my book to see a sur-
prising sight—a carriage was just entering
the park-gates, and I watched it roll along
the distant path towards the house. I was
considerably astonished. The county gentry
were few in number in that neighbourhood,

and not wont to visit my father, in his widowed state, without invitation. It was not, however, so very remarkable a circumstance as to impel me to descend from my perch to inquire into it. Something else that I witnessed half-an-hour later, occurring in the pets' field, which adjoined the apple-orchard, had more effect—it brought me down from the apple-tree, and sent me in flying haste to demand justice from the master.

My father was not in the morning-room, nor in the library ; but, as I ran upstairs, the door of the white drawing-room, a sacred, magnificent apartment, stood open, and I hurried in. The master sat full in the light of a window, and I saw him at once.

'Oh, father !' I exclaimed, full of my grievance, 'Charlie has just been and taken two of my little pigs. He says they are his, because they have a black spot, but some of mine had, too. I know he won't give them

back without you speak to him. And HE
LIFTED THEM OUT OF MY STYE BY THEIR EARS,
SIR! I was up in the apple-tree, and I saw
him do it. My poor old sow did squeak so!'

CHAPTER II.

' My dear Lynton ! Whoever is this ?'

My eyes travelled in amazed search for the speaker. They found her, a lady, magnificent both in size and attire, seated on a couch a little in the shadow. Flowing draperies, gigantic headgear, and massive and haughty features, expressive at this moment of the most utter astonishment, had their due effect upon me. I stood motionless, too abashed even to retire.

My father transferred the reply to me.

' This is your aunt, Mrs. Marshall Abbott, Harry. Come and shake hands with her, and tell her whom you are.'

I advanced to the stately lady, having re-
gained, in this little pause, a fitting amount
of self-possession. My new aunt prepared to
receive me graciously ; she did hold out her
hand, and permitted me to imprint the shape
of mine, in the grime of the apple-tree's
trunk, upon her delicate grey glove. But
she palpably shrunk from bringing my whole
form into contact with her garments.

'And which of my little nephews are you?'
she inquired, with gracious condescension.

'I am Harry, ma'am,' I replied, naturally
repeating to my aunt the name by which I
was known to all my equals, rather than that
hitherto used by servants alone.

'Harry!' said Mrs. Marshall, contracting
her brows just a little in momentary bewilderment, 'Harry!' Then light dawned upon
her memory : 'Surely, my dear Lynton, this
is never your daughter Henrietta?'

My father looked very stern—this was probably the first time he had been compelled to recognise my girlhood since my mother's death.

'Answer your aunt's question, Harry,' he said to me, in an irritated tone.

'Yes, ma'am,' I said, 'I am Henrietta.'

Mrs. Marshall positively rose from her seat, in her bewilderment, and moved a few steps away to survey her niece. That unfortunate child, long-trousered, short-petticoated, and masculine-haired, with sunburnt face, and apple-tree-trunkish hands and clothes, stood to be viewed, very thoroughly conscious of the immense difference between herself and her critic, and suspicious, for the first time in her life, that trousers on a girl might be criminal.

'How old are you, Henrietta?' inquired the lady, when she had mastered every detail of the picture before her.

'I am ten, ma'am.'

'And you—you always look like that—
you wear a dress like that every day ?'

'Yes, ma'am.'

'And this is your only daughter, Mr.
Abbott ?' said his sister-in-law.

'Poor Harry ! What is there objection-
able in the unfortunate fellow ?' said my
father, good-breeding suppressing the annoyance which I saw working at the corner
of his lips.

'Excuse me—I do not want to be intru-
sive,' said Mrs. Marshall, 'but what do you
think poor Catherine would feel if she could
see this child growing up in this manner ?'

I had never seen the master so powerfully
and obviously affected as he was by this mention of his dead wife. Mrs. Marshall Abbott
evidently had diplomatic ability. By this
speech she had prepared my father to listen
to her as, probably, she could not have done
in any other way. Her next sentence was

directed to making him listen good-temperedly.

'I hope my teaching will not have been such as anyone could disapprove,' was my father's reply, but given in a defensive instead of an aggressive tone.

'Indeed, I do not doubt that. But, Lynton, that is not all.' The dean's majestic lady walked forward to the window, dragging her heavy skirts with a rustling noise, and faced my father, with her gloved hand resting gently on his arm, the while she delivered the remainder of her sentence : 'If you are not prepared to listen to and appreciate reason, you are not the Lynton Abbott I knew twenty years ago, when we were all young together.'

This was the most gross flattery. Twenty years before, when the dean and my father were young men at Oxford, and this lady was the daughter of one of the houses where they visited most, I have heard this very Mrs.

Marshall herself declare that she and the dean often laughed together at the way in which the heir of Apsleigh clung to a decision which he had once made, however mistaken or insufficient the grounds upon which he had formed it. But never mind, now. Mrs. Marshall had attained her purpose — the master was thus brought into a pliable condition.

'You cannot alter facts, Lynton,' she went on. 'And what is the very thing for boys will not answer in training girls. This is your only daughter. She is Miss Abbott of Apsleigh; she must take the place of her mother in your household in a few years. However you may insist upon educating her as a boy, she has to be a woman. You cannot make a lady of your daughter in these circumstances.'

'My children are taught to be scrupulously polite to one another,' said my father, a little

frigidly ; ' you would never hear or see rudeness from one to another.'

' Yes,' resumed Mrs. Marshall, undaunted,
' but it is the manner, the *je ne sais quoi*, that
I mean. Now you,' (insidious flattery again)
' you, yourself, Lynton, are one of the most
finished gentlemen I ever knew ; but your
manner would have been strange, indeed,
upon your wife or upon me. It is the
peculiar indefinite something that ¯marks
the lady of which I speak.'

My father unwillingly admitted the force
of this representation.

' Lend me your daughter for a few years,'
said my aunt kindly ; ' I will send her
back to you worthy her position—the only
daughter of the elder branch of our house."

The master's countenance presented a singular mixture of pain, indecision, and gratitude—at least, so I now read the expression
which imprinted itself upon my memory by

its singularity. After a few moments he transferred the question to me :

' Will you go with your Aunt Marshall to be made a lady, Harry ?'

' No, sir, please,' replied I, promptly.

They both smiled at the readiness of my answer ; but I had heard the whole discussion, and slowness of decision was not one of my characteristics.

' I thoroughly appreciate the kindness of your offer, my dear Mrs. Marshall,' said my father, taking up the thread of the discourse, ' but I am very unwilling to part with Harry, and you see he is perfectly certain he doesn't want to go. Is it not all right at present ? Can things not go on very well as they are for some time longer, and the polish be applied later in life ?'

' I find my niece dressed in—yes, in BOYS' clothes,' replied Mrs. Marshall solemnly, ' with her hair parted at the side, and her face and hands stained extraordinary colours ; and she presents herself to me by saying something about her pigstye ! This is when she is ten years old. No, Mr. Abbott ! It must *not* be delayed any longer. If your daughter is to be fitted for her station in society, the beginning of the work is already too long deferred. How is she ever to . . . Run away a little while, Henrietta, my child, while I talk to your papa.'

She paused in her argument until I had left the room. I departed to the library, where I sat with my hands clenched, and my thoughts a perfect whirl of anger and dismay. The possibility of complete change and severance from all that I had loved through all my life, which had opened before me as suddenly as a gulf before the feet of the victim of an earthquake, was so appalling that I was momentarily unable to realise it in all its dreadful significance.

Nearly half an hour must have passed when I heard the drawing-room bell ring ; and presently after my father's voice bidding the housemaid to tell Stillingfleet that Mrs. Abbott would dine with him at six, and also to send nurse to him. When nurse's step sounded along the passage and up the stairs, I could not resist the temptation to steal to the door, that I might listen what should be said to her—for was I not then to hear my fate declared ?

'Mrs. Marshall Abbott is kindly going to take Harry on a visit, nurse,' I heard my father say ; 'you must put such things as you think will be of use to him—to—her, and her books, and so on, into a trunk. She will leave about half-past six this evening.'

'And nurse,' said Mrs. Marshall's voice, 'I suppose Miss Henrietta has a dress made in the ordinary fashion—not like what she has on just now ?'

'Miss Hetty only haves two longish frocks, ma'am ; one white, and one blue French merino, which she wears when the master haves visitors. I'm very sorry, ma'am,' said nurse, ' as I didn't catch her to put one on afore you saw her.'

' And they are really fit to be seen, are they? Well, will you be good enough to put on her the merino, and you need not pack any such dresses as she has on now.'

Mrs. Marshall having gained my father's irrevocable word, was carrying things with rather a high hand.

I rushed out of the library, out of the house, in a perfect agony of grief and apprehension. My three brothers, returning from Apsleigh—for Charley had gone, after juggling with the pigs, to meet George and Willie—found me in my crushing anguish. I had gathered around me the dearly-loved creatures from whom I was about to be separated for ever. I had laid my head upon the shaggy side of my great New-foundland, and Crisp, my woolly-haired mongrel, nestled his faithful body within an outstretched arm; gathered into my lap were my guinea-pig, and my favourite white rab-bit; and upon his perch in the aviary, where my longing, upturned eyes rested upon him, sat the handsome clever parrot, who was the delight and pride of my life. These made up half my world. I was doomed to bid them an eternal farewell! No fears for my own future entered my mind; every thought was absorbed by the coming wrench of parting from these, and then from Willie and my father—in a word, from all that my heart contained.

'Poor dear Harry! What is the matter?' cried Willie, kneeling down and tenderly substituting his shoulder for Alexander's side.

The convulsive sobs, which were redoubled at this action, prevented me from speaking, for the time; but I moved my burning eyes from the parrot, and turned them upon my best-loved brother.

'Poor dear old fellow,' said Willie anxiously, ' can't you say what it is ?'

I struggled to reply, but my voice seemed entirely gone. Fortunately, at this moment nurse came, with red eyes, in search of the victim, to dress it for sacrifice on the altar of conventionality. Willie appealed to her for an explanation.

'Miss Hetty's going to be taken away from us all, to go with her aunt, at a moment's notice,' said nurse, indignantly.

With a mighty shudder, breath returned to me at this blunt statement of my cruel fate.

'Oh ! Willie, Willie !' I gasped, throwing my arms round his neck, ' I cannot go away ! I shall die, I shall die !'

CHAPTER III.

I was very weary when, on the evening of the day following my sudden separation from my home treasures, my aunt, her maid, and I, alighted from the train at the station of the cathedral town of Dalestonbury. The plump carriage which had come to meet us received as one of its occupants an unfortunate little girl, sick with mental and bodily fatigue. We had travelled far into the middle of the night to reach London, and I had lain in the hotel bed, kept awake by misery for many hours, only falling into a doze from sheer exhaustion a little while before my aunt's maid came to dress me for breakfast. Weary hours of travelling had been again undergone, and at last, at five in the evening, we reached the Lincolnshire town where was to be my present place of rest.

All through the early part of the journey, my only relief from sorrow had been strong resentment against Mrs. Marshall, who appeared to me in the guise of a bitter, cruel enemy. But grief gradually subdued me. My aunt, finding me silent, had wisely spoken to me very little. And now I was prepared to feel even grateful for her kindness when she drew me back into the cushions of the carriage, and, resting my head on her shoulder, told me encouragingly that we had nearly reached our journey's end.

Through nearly a mile of the principal street of the town, then for a few minutes past high, grey walls, above which I saw the

cathedral church rising; then the carriage
passed through large iron gates, opened by
the footman, and we dashed along a short
avenue, bordering the lawn, up to the door
of the Deanery.

The Rev. Dr. Marshall Abbott, Dean of
Dalestonbury, Rector of Haughton and Upper Fifley, author of 'Notes on the Athana-
sian Creed,' and numerous other works—this
dignitary was the elderly, thin, grave gentleman who stood in the drawing-room door to
receive us; and who, after greeting his wife,
turned upon my figure a look of amazement—
almost incredulity.

' Who is this little lady?' he asked.

' She is Miss Abbott,' said his wife, calmly;
evidently it did not strike her that he might
desire to express an opinion upon her action
with respect to me.

' What!—Lynton's only daughter?'

' Just so—but don't keep me to explain

now. We are both thoroughly tired, and we must dress a little for dinner. Come with me, Henrietta.'

I followed her up the stairs to a pretty little sanctum, half dressing-room, half boudoir. Here Mrs. Marshall submitted herself to the hands of Parks, and emerged with a wonderful coronet of hair; then she was attired in a violet, lace-adorned robe, far outstripping in splendour the black silk in which she had visited my father. Never once, through all the fifteen years of their wedded life, had Mrs. Abbott taken her seat at the head of the dean's table without first performing an elaborate toilette, without bracelets on her fine arms, and diamond earrings glittering be side her hair. And, in return, never had the dean's eyes, even, much less his heart, strayed for one moment from their legitimate object of admiration.

Parks exerted all her skill, and expended a

considerable quantity of pomade upon my favoured head.

'Really, ma'am,' she was constrained to say at last, 'I don't know what is to be done with the young lady's hair. It's too short to tie back with a ribbon, and lie down parted in the middle it won't! It stands up bolt, ma'am. I'll have to part it at the side.'

My aunt surveyed me for a moment with a dissatisfied face. Then she said :

'Certainly it cannot be allowed to stand up in that absurd fashion. So it must be parted at the side, to begin with. That is only one of many things we will alter by degrees.'

The clanging of the dinner-bell had hastened her decision, and we had only just entered the drawing-room when the butler announced, 'Dinner is served, sir.'

My aunt had not dropped my hand after descending the stairs, and now she took the dean's arm on the other side, and thus led me into the dining-room. By this means I was prevented from seeing the other person who was coming to dinner.

The brilliant light, and the splendour of the table, dazzled me for the moment. My father lived simply, and the family plate was only produced on those rare occasions when he had visitors, and then we children were kept out of the way. The dean's wife approved of a showy table, as much as of a showy person. Silver forks and spoons daily would never content her. The useless metal glittered under the gas, which the dusk of the October evening made necessary; and the heart of the butler, whose was the responsibility, and the fingers of the footman, whose was the labour, had never a day's respite, whether visitors came to the Deanery, or whether the display shone under the eyes of its mistress alone.

We stood at the table while the dean delivered himself of grace. My irreverent eyes, straying over the flowers in the épergne, saw, at the other side of the great table, a tall bony youth, at vision of whom my heart beat.

'Ah, Marshall,' said Mrs. Abbott, as she raised her eyes, 'where were you when I came in ?   Can you guess who this little girl is ?'

He looked at me from under his eyebrows. I thought he was scowling, but it was natural to him.

'No, ma'am.'   Answer given with a kind of sulky indifference.

'It is your little sister Henrietta.   You will like to have home news from her.   No, my child, sit still now ; you can talk to your brother after dinner.'

A gleam of interest in the bony youth's eye had made me, impulsive, start up to go toward him.   On this same youth I built all my hopes of immediate happiness.

During the progress of dinner the dean

and his wife talked at intervals on local
affairs. The sullen youth said never a word
the whole time; either his faculties were
absorbed by his feeding, or he was trained to
chew the cud of his own observations in
silence. It was not until the servants departed, leaving the dessert on the table, that
Mrs. Marshall proceeded to give the promised
explanation of my presence.

'As I wrote to you I intended,' she said,
addressing the dean, ' I went a little out of
my way to Exeter station, and drove from
there to Abbey Castle. Of course, Lynton
was surprised to see me, but he was exceedingly cordial. He told me the children were
all out; and no doubt he meant to have
them duly prepared for presentation to me.
But this young lady came rushing into the
room with some information about her pigstye. And really, when I discovered that it
was Henrietta, I was horrified ; my dear dean,

I won't make her blush by describing her appearance. But you could never have guessed she wasn't a boy ; and a very untidy one, too. Lynton called her "Harry," and, it seemed to me, never made the slightest difference in his treatment of them between her and the rest of his boys. Did you know that your father was bringing up this girl in such an out-of-the-way fashion, Marshall ?'

The saturnine youth was smiling a heavy smile. He aroused at this direct question, and answered, gruffly as briefly—

' Yes, ma'am.'

' Why did you never speak about it to me ? Then we might have taken some steps about it before.'

' It was not my place to interfere with what the master saw fit to do '—relapsing into complete gloom again.

' You mistake, Marshall,' said the dean, in a tutorial tone ; ' it is the bounden duty of every person to interfere to prevent abuse of power.'

This doctrine of universal interference did not please his wife.

'Nonsense,' she interposed, 'Marshall talks reasonably. His excuse is a good one. Of course, it is not his place to interfere with or criticise the judgments and decisions of his elders. Remember always what you have just said, Marshall.'

Marshall's brows lowered as much more as it was physically possible for them to do. Surveying him, I opined that his aunt's words and his front together implied that the doctrine was one not always practically supported by him. But therein I under-rated the young man's craftiness.

'But really,' continued Mrs. Marshall, 'this state of affairs was nothing to be laughed over. It would have been deplorable if the only daughter of the elder family had been brought up right to womanhood in this strange manner. The poor girl would have been a social monstrosity, of no possible use in creation. I felt that it was only Christian charity—only my duty to my husband's name—to rescue her from this fate. No doubt, dean, you will agree with me?'

Mrs. Marshall was far too clever a woman, and had far too much self-respect, to possess a hen-pecked husband. What glory can a woman find in the submission of her husband to her judgment, when it is patent to all the world that his deference is mere homage of fear? What compliment to her wisdom is there, when it is evident to all who have eyes to see that her counsel is followed by her lord merely because he has a constitutional desire for a quiet life? The utmost respect for her husband's opinion was always shown by the Dean's wife. No step of importance was definitely taken by her without his concurrence. But the remarkable point was that never in public, and, so far as could be known, never in private, was there a difference of intention or opinion between them; and Mrs. Marshall was certain of her husband's approbation for whatever she took in hand.

This result had not been obtained by the rough means which stupid women put in force. Mrs. Abbott had never coaxed her legal master; still less had she at any period bullied her liege. Not one storm of wrath, not one whirlwind of undignified hysteria, had swept across the calm sea of their joined life.

Such ruses as these are the resources of weak minds. Mrs. Marshall Abbott was not weak. In all the essential points of strength of character she was the superior of her husband. The firmer, broader intellect was his; the rapidity and tenacity of decision, the

clearness of perception, the perseverance, the
readiness of judgment, were hers. Thus the
administrative ability belonged to her, and
the seals of office came to her hand unasked
for. Whosoever must cry aloud for power,
by the act proves himself unworthy thereof.

The little world of Dalestonbury could
not analyse them mentally, to know this;
between themselves it had never been acknowledged, even to silent consciousness. It
never is. Our friends and relatives have their
standing places in our minds—our equals, our
superiors, our inferiors; but they are classified
by unconscious cerebration, and acknowledged
unknowingly.

Therefore the Dean scarcely felt that he
always submitted to his wife; therefore the
gossips of their world could not understand
why he did so. Nine times out of ten, when
the Dean had heard his wife's opinion, he
simply altered her vocabulary, and returned

her one of her own sentences in sounding language, under the honest impression that it was an original production of his own thought. So did he now ; for he answered her question thus :

' I do agree with you, quite. Poor little one ! she would have been devoid of purpose and position in life—there would have been no local habitation in society discoverable for such a *lusus naturæ*. You have exhibited your customary benevolence and perspicacity, my love.'

I must defend myself, *en avance*, from being supposed to convey that these reflections upon the character and position of this reverend doctor and his lady were those of a child of ten. By no means. Precocious and early strong-minded as I was, I had not quite got up to that point. But when I call up these vivid remembrances of my early days, you must expect to find them sometimes alloyed

4—2

or refined by the matured understanding
through which I must draw them. The intelligence of later years casts a new light
upon the remembered facts of earlier years.
One has no choice but to present the facts of
one's early years more or less embellished by
their setting in the wisdom of maturity ; the
character of the fact is not altered by the
surroundings.

'I am afraid,' added Mrs. Marshall, by
way of concluding the subject, 'that
Henrietta does not see me in the light of
a benefactress, at present. She was very
grieved to part from her brothers—especially
from the big fair boy, the eldest at home.
Then there were a number of pet animals
which it was a great grief to lose. In fact,
we have had to bring one particularly ugly
little dog, named Crisp, with us, in a basket ;
for poor Henrietta's heart-strings were twined
around him so closely that they would have

been broken if he had been left behind. Never mind, darling,' benevolently patting my shoulder as she rose from table, 'you will understand one day what a fortunate event for you this is.'

CHAPTER IV.

When we re-entered the drawing-room after dinner, my aunt, having first required and received an assurance that I was not sleepy, and added on her side a caution that she should not permit me to sit up later than eight, referred me for amusement to a table covered with books.

She and my uncle sat down, immediately under the chandelier, to play cribbage. The evening was the only leisure time that the Dean permitted himself; cribbage and back-gammon were his beau-ideals of healthy mental recreative games, and his wife duti-fully resigned herself for several hours each evening to assisting him in obtaining this same recreation.

The books failed to interest me. The truth was, I was thoroughly fagged out, but possessed in perfection the boyish reluctance to acknowledge overpowering fatigue. I glanced at all the books near by me ; then got up from my seat and went to the other side of the table, to inspect those there. Thus I stood with my back to my aunt for a moment. I heard her call my name in her clear tones. I went to her.

'My child,' she said, 'you must stand straight. You are pushing one shoulder farther than the other out of that frock.'

This unjust accusation was a little irritating. I was rather proud of my straight figure, which my father had been wont to praise. I rebelled.

' I was not, indeed, ma'am.'

'One shoulder was higher up than the other, Henrietta.'

'But my pocket is on that side.'

'Do you mean that there is something in your pocket so heavy that it drags down your dress from your shoulder ?   What is it ?'

'I have my pocket-knife, ma'am.'

'Show it to me, my child.'

I produced the knife obediently—the knife which Willie had brought for me from the blacksmith at Apsleigh, and which he had forgotten to give me until my trunk was corded.

Mrs. Marshall drew her brows a little together when I exhibited my possession.

'It is no wonder that your dress is dragged down,' was her comment.   'That great thing is utterly unfit for a girl.   You are to be a boy no longer, Henrietta—go and offer that knife to your brother.'

For a variety of reasons this command was

not congenial to my feelings. The knife had considerable intrinsic value in my eyes; it was one of the few mementoes that I possessed of my past happy life. It was the last thing that Willie's hand had touched, the memorial of the last little service his brotherly affection had wrought for me. I felt that I was beginning to undergo a kind of persecution, and anger spoke in my tones.

'My father had it made on purpose for me, ma'am.'

'Very possibly; but——'

'And it has a dissecting blade,' I interrupted.

'Then Marshall will like it so much the more. He takes a great interest in that sort of study. But you do not require a dissecting blade now. You must not dispute my commands, my dear child.'

My uncle by this time had finished redealing the cards; and, with an air of leaving the point completely settled, Mrs. Marshall returned to her game.

This kind of dogmatic authority over my personal trivial affairs was new to me, and anything but pleasant. If my aunt had continued to argue the point, I should have continued to resist; but the calmness with which she closed the conversation quite overpowered my speech.

The option of silent resistance—that is, disobedience—remained to me. Under other circumstances, judging by my character, I probably should have taken this course— should have defiantly disregarded the arbitrary command. At this moment the force of my self-will was lessened by extreme fatigue, and, in addition, I presently found that I had a reason of my own for obeying the order.

I leant my back against the table thinking the matter over. The lowering youth sat at

an occasional table, right at the other end of
the room ; with a tall dismal-looking volume
supported in front of him, to catch the full
light of the wax candles on the bracket behind him. He seemed absorbed in his book ;
all emotions, from amusement down to disgust,
expressed themselves on his countenance by
the one expedient of bringing lower his brows,
already unpleasantly overhanging. His eyes,
now, were apparently as far back as his ears.
He did not look inviting, by any means.

But this penthouse-browed youth was my
brother, and I wanted him to love. The remembrance that I was to find him in this
strange place had been my one sustaining
thought all through the misery I had endured. The bleeding fibres of my heart,
yearning for something to cling to in comfort
for their lost supports, were yet not indis-
criminating. They were not prepared to clasp
the first persons whom they encountered.

Mrs. Marshall had been the cause of their agony; the Dean, as I opined, was learned and stern; no servant here had the claim of association and fidelity on my affection. I had known I could not yet love any of these. But I was to find a brother here. The name had for me only a sweet significance. It was the drop of syrup in the bitter cup—Hope at the bottom of the box.

That is to say, this dark, gloomy, thick-browed, heavy, and altogether unpleasant young person, who had not addressed one word to his lonely little sister, was my syrup, my Hope !

It occurred to me, at once, that the delivering up to him of one of my few treasures was the best of opportunities for enticing forth for my delight this young gentleman's syrupy qualities. Besides, I would not object to yielding anything whatever to this brother, on whom all my yearning love was to be concentrated. I would obey, certainly.

I opened all the blades, having in view his full appreciation of the gift, when I had arrived at this consoling determination, and went gently along the room to act upon it.

My soft short skirts and my light weight moved noiselessly over the thick carpet. It was not until my shadow fell upon his page that my syrup observed my approach. Instantly he caught a thin yellow-covered pamphlet up from the leaves of the divinity volume and huddled it under his loosely-spread handkerchief, the while his face became of a pale violet hue. Then he looked up, and disappointedly remarked to me that I was only myself.

'Aunt sent me,' I commenced; this was very far indeed from the beginning I had intended to make, but he looked so sour that I felt constrained to offer a kind of apology for

my presumption in disturbing him. 'Aunt
sent me to give you this knife.'

The light glittered upon the open blades,
and his eyes, from out their cavern, watched
the shining radiance; but his tongue only un-
enthusiastically responded:

'Um—m?'

'She said you would like to have it,' I
added, doubtful if he understood his good
fortune.

'Well? Why don't you put it down?'

'Aren't you even going to say "Thank
you"?' I demanded indignantly.

'Bosh! Thank you, child.'

He was impatient to resume his surrepti-
tious yellow-covered book—his hand twitched
upon it under the handkerchief; as a hint to
that effect, he devoted his regards to the great
work which he appeared, from the distance,
to be so absorbed in. But I could not quite
resign my Hope all in a moment. My small

flash of indignation went out, and I ventured, with my heart in my tones, another innocent remark :

' You are my brother Marshall, aren't you ?'

' Yes,' in dreary voice.

' Will you take me about with you ?'

' No.' In precisely the same tone.

' Won't you be very fond of me ?'

' I can't say.'

Upon this crusher I subsided, and stood before him silent. Only so for one instant ; then he raised his eyes from the depths, and said :

' Go away. I cannot read with you there.'

Even as I turned to obey him the small book came forth again.

How can I describe the emotions of that moment, in which the last gleam of light in my heavens faded out, and the blackness of desolation reigned overhead ? A feeling of

utter, utter solitude overwhelmed my soul.
In the midst of a desert, craving for the
sound of human voice, for the touch of human
hand, longing to kiss ground upon which
another human being's foot had stepped, the
miserable castaway could not feel more
fearfully alone than I in Dean Abbott's drawing-room. Who can realise this sorrowful
moment with my memory? They only who,
with similar circumstances, have known the
torture of possessing a heart at once proud
and warm.

When my aunt sent me up to bed, misery
broke through my reserve, and I piteously
implored Parks to bring up Crisp from the
kitchen for a few moments. When the good-
natured young woman complied, and my
dearly-loved doggie came bounding around
me, testifying his delight by the ardour of
his caresses, I obtained some relief; for, clasping him in my arms, I sat down upon the

ground, and buried in his woolly neck the bitter sensation of lovelessness.

The next day, the course of my immediate education was begun. My aunt, inquiring what I knew most about, and being answered ' Latin and anatomy,' was horrified.

Her corrective measures commenced by setting me down at once to an hour's drudgery at the piano under her tuition, and getting in hand two elaborate fancy-work undertakings. There was a shopping expedition, too ; and I suffered the pain of being turned round and round by a dressmaker for an hour, in process of making several new frocks.

These proceedings occupied most of the day. In the evening, books were my only amusement. My brother Marshall seemed occupied all day, either studying with the Dean, or assisting in the cathedral service, or following his own devices ; and in the even-

ing, when he was in the drawing-room, he
ensconced himself in silence behind some great
work—I always suspected that big book,
though. He never spoke one word of kindness to me; never made an effort to relieve
the monotony of my leisure moments. He
might have won from me, then, devotion
which would have lasted all through our
lives; as it was, I lived upon the memory of
Willie and my father, with the present affection and comfort of Crisp.

Things had progressed in this manner for a
week, when, one morning, it occurred to my
aunt that the small trunk brought with me
from home had not yet been opened; and
when I was released from drumming over
the lines and spaces, and notes 'above the
clef,' she summoned me to my bedroom to
assist in the unpacking.

We had nearly reached the bottom of the
box—Mrs. Marshall having, with calm con-

tempt, presented to Parks most of the garments it contained—when we came to a very large book. I pounced upon it, and affectionately hugged its covers.

'What is that book, my dear?' Mrs. Abbott asked.

'Ellis's Anatomy, aunt;' she had forbidden me to call her 'ma'am.'

'Dear me! Why was that packed for you, I wonder?'

The question was not interrogative of me, but I answered at once :

'Because I have learnt lessons out of it. I've gone straight through the bones and muscles, nearly; and I know a lot about the other part, too. Oh, it is so interesting, aunt! Willie and I learnt together out of this book every day, and dear Willie ran to ask the master if he would get him another one, that I might take this and keep up with Willie—learn as much as he would do, every day. I shall have a whole chapter to catch up now.'

I was voluble with satisfaction, and beamed upon the big volume.

Mrs. Abbott's answer came in those calm, finished tones which I was learning to hate and dread :

' I am sorry to be constantly reminding you, dear child, that you have come with me on purpose *not* to do all the peculiar things you did at home. Willie studies anatomy because he is going to be a doctor ; you are going to be no such thing, and you must not study a subject utterly useless, and even improper, for a girl.'

' Even improper for a girl.' Mrs. Marshall, with all her strong common-sense, was not emancipated sufficiently to think about such a matter for herself. And I was not able to ask her, What is the guilt in the name of a bone ? What propriety is outraged

by the mention of the designation of a
muscle? How, even, does it injure the deli-
cacy and modesty of a girl to know the
probable weight of her liver or brain? How
will it hurt her to understand the needs of
her own digestive and respiratory apparatus?
How, above all, can it be possible for any
natural operation to be 'improper?'

Even if I could have asked her authorita-
tively all these pertinent questions, she would
probably have been deafened to any consideration but the word of 'Society.' So, with
a harsh phrase, are the noblest children of
this world ruled; and who will dare assert
that they are yet wiser than the children of
light?

'It is quite suitable for Marshall,' was the
only reply my eager protestations and en-
treaties could obtain. 'He is much interested
in the subject, and I do not see fit to interfere with him, although it is not his particular

study. Now, Henrietta, do not make me cross; take that book to your brother, at once. Let me see,' consulting her watch; 'he is just now free from the Dean, and he passes the whole of his leisure time in his laboratory—you will find him there. You must go through the kitchen-garden, and down a narrow path at the extreme left-hand corner. Tap at the door, and say I sent you. Go at once, my dear.'

The impression made upon me by Marshall's behaviour the first evening of my arrival had somewhat passed off. If he took an interest in medical subjects, so did I—and this bond of union must go some way toward making him like me. He was 'in his laboratory,' too; perhaps there was something there which might interest me. On the whole, I felt not unwilling to go in search of my brother, even though the object of that search was the yielding up of my treasured volume.

I went to the passage leading to the kitchen, and called Crisp—I dared not whistle for him—and my only friend and I started off down the path together.

Crisp was overjoyed to see me; he always was, poor fellow. I suspect he moped a little in my absence. But when he did get me, he enjoyed it the more. He frisked about, shaking his bushy tail almost out of its socket, and uttering expressive yelps of impulsive delight.

We duly found the large outhouse which was appropriated to Marshall's private study. Certainly, his aunt was mistaken when she said he passed the whole of his leisure time there, for he was not there now. I doubt very much if Mrs. Marshall knew in the least how the greater part of his time was spent.

However, just as I was about to give him up, and go back with my book to report the fact to my aunt, he returned. The young gentleman had been out of the Deanery grounds, for he came scrambling up the wall, out of the field which was beyond the kitchen-garden. He put his head over the wall to reconnoitre; I immediately hailed him, and he, after hanging there a moment to delibe-rate, concluded to come over and face me.

I presume that the outward cordiality of the reception I received from him was a course dictated by policy. At all events, he certainly did look no more scowlingly than he could help, and even gave me, for the first time, a cold insincere kiss, before he asked me what I wanted.

'Aunt told me to come here,' I informed him, 'and give you my " Ellis's Anatomy." She says she won't let me study it, and you are fond of it; but so am I.'

'Thank you,' he said, taking the book. Then, after a moment's pause, he added, insinuatingly, 'I say, Harry, do you like learning anatomy ?'

'That I do !' I returned, overjoyed at the mere possibility which this question seemed to open. 'Oh, Marshall ! will you show me some of your books, and bones ?'

'This is a dissecting-room,' said he, impressively, then waited.

'The master used to let us get sheep's hearts, and things like that, at home,' said I 'Aren't they curious ?'

'Would you like to come in it ?' he asked, unheeding my interruption.

'Yes, please !'

'Well, then — Harry,' sinking his voice, 'promise not to tell aunt that I wasn't here when you came, and I will take you in, and show you my museum.'

'Oh ! of course, I won't tell her,' I promised readily enough.

'You are quite sure—even if she asks you?'

'Yes, quite. I don't tell stories, Marshall.'

Hereupon he opened the door with a small key, produced from his pocket, and he, Crisp, and I, passed in together.

The place was boarded, and had whitewashed walls. There were no windows in the side, so that the room could not be pried into from without; but a large skylight admitted a sufficient quantity of light. There were shelves on one side, filled with a number of large glass bottles, containing various preparations. Marshall was amiable enough—for a purpose—to walk along the shelves with me, explaining to me the contents of some of the bottles. There was another large shelf filled with books.

My father made Marshall the same liberal allowance that he had granted each of his sons at school; so that my brother was able to gratify this taste, expensive as it was.

My unfeigned interest and attention discovered the softest corner of Marshall's hard
nature. He became quite friendly, and even
communicative to me, when he discovered
how much I knew, and how truthfully I en
joyed knowing. He was nearly eighteen
now, and had been sent to his uncle directly
after his fourteenth birthday, when I was
only seven. He knew very little, therefore,
about me; and was a good deal astonished
by what he was discovering.

' How came you to begin to learn all this ?'
he asked, at length.

' Willie and I learnt together,' I replied;
' we are both going to be doctors.'

' Why, *you* can't, you little stupid,' interposed my brother.

' Can't I ? Why not? '

' Why, you are a girl.'

' Oh dear ! I wish I wasn't !' a wish I repeated many times after. ' Aunt says so,

too, but father always set Willie and me tasks together. Why are girls never doctors ?'

To this question no reasonable reply could be given ; and Marshall's only attempt thereat was—

'Because—they never are. And did the master let you ever cut up anything ?' he added.

'Oh yes!' I replied ; 'that knife that I gave you, he had made on purpose for me, that it might have a long thin dissecting blade.'

Marshall produced the knife from his pocket, and began to examine it, blade by blade. It was a very great knife, the largest blade being nine or ten inches long. I felt no pang of envy as he looked it all over. My only struggle had been at first ; the decision to resign it quietly once arrived at, I did not waste further regret upon it.

'And how came you to study ?' I asked,

as he stood thus occupied. ' *You* are not going to be a doctor, you know.'

' No,' he said ; and his brow clouded down ; the moody expression returned to his countenance, his voice took another tone. ' No ; but I ought to be. It is all my interest—all my pleasure. I have talent for this work which will be completely wasted as a priest. What right has my father to force us into whatever profession he happens to choose.'

Here he caught sight of my wondering face ; and the repression to which he was habituated resumed its sway. He gave a little laugh, as though in scorn of himself for being betrayed into expression ; then turned his back to me, and stood quite still, looking apparently at the open blade.

Crisp at this moment called my attention by a little yelp. He had been running up and down, and had found his way into a chamber of horrors. The end of the place was boarded off, and some sacking was hung up to form a kind of door. Through this Crisp had penetrated; through this I followed him —suspecting no wrong—when I heard his little cry.

Another instant, and I was back at the aperture.

'Oh, Marshall, Marshall!' I cried, forget ting, in my excitement, that he was the very person who must know all about it. 'Here are four poor little frogs, on a table, with drawing-pins through their legs, and cut about so dreadfully, and ALIVE! Oh! do come and kill them, poor little creatures; please do!'

His eyes went back into their depths, and he became that deep violet colour which I had seen his face once before.

'Come away from there,' he growled.

But my eyes had grown accustomed to the comparative obscurity of this place, and

I saw yet more—an unfortunate dog, on whom, I suppose, the action of a poison was being tried by my tender-hearted brother.

'And there is a poor dog here,' I continued, excited and pitying. 'It is dying in awful agony—it's too bad to speak. Crisp, Crisp! do keep away. Oh, it is writhing so horribly! Marshall, do, do come and put it out of misery!'

Marshall came; but for no such purpose. He came to lay his hands on my shoulders to move me away from the sight. I caught hold of the boards and implored him, myself in an agony of grief and rage, to mercifully kill his victims. He was very strong, this bony youth; he quickly overpowered me, and lifted me through the aperture—then stood looking down upon me, with a glare in his far-away eyes.

'Marshall, do kill them!' I begged.

'I shall not,' he said, slowly.

' I'm sure aunt doesn't know,' I cried. ' I will go straight and tell her !'

' You will do no such thing,' he said, rousing himself at this, and grasping my arm painfully.

' I will !' reiterated I, with the firmness of a martyr.

' You shan't !' he said, with a fearful deliberateness. ' I will keep you locked up here until you promise not to say a word about it to anyone. You had no right to go in there.'

' Aunt knows where I am,' I retorted. ' She will send to look for me at luncheon-time.'

' I will murder you, if you do not promise !' he said between his teeth. But, through it all, his countenance remained fixed in calm stolidity. While I blazed in my fury, his wrath was the white heat of burning metal. Only his eyes flamed far away, his skin kept that violet hue, and his teeth were tightly set.

' No ; you won't murder me,' said I, indignation extinguishing all prudence ; ' because if you do you will be hanged, and you will be afraid of that. Cruel people are always cowards !'

He released my arm, which his grasp had completely benumbed, so suddenly that the quick rush of the blood made me scream perforce, and caught up poor little Crisp, who was barking in amazement. In an instant my brother had clutched me again, this time by the hair, and, holding my poor dog up as high as he could, again demanded a promise of my silence. Personal ill-usage only had the result of increasing my determination. But the imploring eyes of my loved dog—my only friend and intimate in this place—fixed upon me, sobered me. I tried to come to terms.

'Will you promise not to do anything more like that?' I asked.

'No,' said Marshall, with a sneer, 'I shall not promise.'

'Then I *will* tell aunt!' said I, firmly.

'Take care,' he hissed, 'because I am going to kill your dog instead of you, if you don't promise.'

'Oh, Marshall!' I exclaimed. 'Put him down. My poor Crisp!'

'Will you promise?'

I did not believe he would really injure my beloved, my darling friend, or I might have given in at once. But I thought of the poor creatures in the next room, and answered desperately :

'I will never promise!'

He lifted my Crisp up to the full height of his arm, immediately he heard my answer, and flung the poor creature with all his strength on to the ground.

' Oh, I won't tell—I won't tell !' I cried, dropping on my knees, as he released his hold on me.

But I was too late. Two great strides over the room, and he reached my open knife ; in an instant, he was back with its long blade bare and gleaming, and sheathed it to the very hilt in the dog's side.

The sharp stab seemed to arouse Crisp from the stunning effect of his fall. He began to utter loud and piercing cries, and to writhe in agony. His poor eyes found me, pre-sently, and seemed mutely reproachful and imploring.

For myself—I cannot tell what I did. I also gave a loud shriek as I saw the dreadful deed ; then my voice, and my remembrance, and consciousness departed together. I went up to him, flung myself on the ground beside him, and lifted his agonised body into my lap. He must have died soon ; for the blood poured from the deep wound. But I cannot in the least guess how long I sat there, stunned, watching the quivers of his dying breaths. When the last one came— when he stretched himself out, and was silent and stiff upon my lap—silent for evermore ! —I have a vague remembrance of seeing Marshall, as through a mist, and far away, placidly wiping his hands upon a towel. Then I know that he came up to me and lifted me right off the ground, and placed me, still grasping my dead pet tightly, on the ground outside his door. Then I know that he locked up his house of mourning, pocketed his key, and walked away, with just the same indifference and gloom upon his sullen face as was commonly there visible.

And I know that I sat upon the ground, gazing with dull glazed eyes upon my dead favourite, for very, very long before tears came to my relief—and for longer still before the servants sent in search of me took away my dead sorrow by force, and led me into the house—and that I will not profane my intense, even if childish emotions, by attempting to describe them in feeble words.

But I know that, from that day, I dreaded my brother Marshall with the dread of an intense horror !

CHAPTER V.

DID you ever hear of that poor man who was
the possessor of a valuable dog, for which he
might have obtained a large sum of money ;
and of how, when that man was starving, a
rich man came to him, and offered him a
great bribe to part with his friend ?

' I will sell you my dog, sir,' said the unfortunate man to his tempter ; ' but there is
one thing I cannot sell you. When you take
him away you must please contrive to leave
me *the wag of his tail !'*

I tell you that story—in which, if you be
so far gifted by nature, you will find infinite
pathos, or over which you may laugh, if you be

insensible enough—to spare myself the thank-
less task of expatiating on my own sorrow
over my murdered dog. I had lost not only
the sight of him, the knowledge of his existence, but also the wag of his tail. Those
who can understand my loss at all will need
that I should add no more. Those who
judge the death of a dog of no account—for
are there not plenty more dogs in the world?
—might hear me talk to them of dumb sympathy, of unfailing affection, of disinterested
devotion, for an hour, and would not understand that ' wag of his tail ' when I had done,
but would kindly pity the childish hyper-sen-
sitiveness of getting hysterical over so slight
a thing as—*just* one dog less in the world !

My aunt had sent to find me that I might
be dressed to go to luncheon, which was my
dinner-time. But Parks decided that I was
only fit to go to bed ; and on her report Mrs.
Abbott came in to see me. She felt my

hands, and looked at my eyes ; called me her 'poor child,' and confirmed Parks' dictum.

So I went to bed, and stayed there, in a low-feverish condition, for the next week— on the fourth day of which the dean and my brother came to my bedside, with Mrs. Marshall. The dean was going on the Continent for the remaining two months of the year ; and my brother was accompanying him on this tour, to obtain the final advantage accruing to him from his eminent relative's guardianship ; when he returned, the preparations for his matriculation at Oxford would be commenced. I accepted dumbly the dean's solemn pat on the head and benediction, but when my brother approached to touch me with his cruel hand, and lay his hypocritical lips on mine, energy awoke, and I buried my head under the clothes.

Mrs. Marshall protested gravely and in vain ; and she was far too wise to insist upon my receiving the unwelcome farewell caress. So my brother Marshall in his boyhood passed out of my sight for ever. Before I saw him again, he had taken the second step in the prints of the feet of his uncle, the dean ; when next I need to write of him, he was M.A., a holy priest, and vicar of the family living at Apsland.

The bishops and pastors of the flock lay hands suddenly on no man, but faithfully and wisely make choice of men with rich fathers. When Marshall Abbott appears in my life and my story again, he will be sanctified by this wise imposition of apostolic hands, which he will have been chosen to receive for three very good and sufficient reasons : *videlicet*—Primus : He was not the eldest son of his father. Secundus : Nevertheless, his father could pay for this younger son the sum of money which is the only essential to ' fitness ' for the sacred ministry. Tertius : There was a living 'in the family,' and 'the family' possessed interest in the disposal of many another ecclesiastical good thing. Could better reasons why Marshall Abbott should duly be given by his bishop authority to remit and retain the sins of his fellow-mortals possibly be imagined ?

When I was sufficiently recovered from my attack of illness to go downstairs again, I found that I had, unconsciously, been occupying a sort of mild Damocles' position. Mrs. Marshall had a lecture in store for me, which she had waited all these days to deliver.

If I might have spoken to my aunt when I saw her immediately after I had been horrified by the sight of Marshall's cruelties, I should probably have poured forth at once the whole story, and implored pity for the sufferers, and vengeance on the criminal. But she, careful for my health, had closed my lips, bidding me not talk about it—by which she meant Crisp's death—until I was better.

Now, in the meanwhile, things altered their aspect in my eyes, in various ways. There was a little speech from Parks, momentarily incautious, for one thing. When she was proceeding to undress me for bed, she saw my arm, and suddenly exclaimed :

'Good gracious! What is the matter with your arm, miss ?'

' I don't know,' I answered wearily : to lie down and be still presented itself at that moment to my eyes as the *summum bonum.* I did not want to tell my affairs to Parks, still less did I covet the labour, an herculean one to me at the best of times, of evading questions. But Parks was undauntable.

' Your arm up at the top is one mask of bruises, poor little thing! Who did it, miss ?'

' Marshall did,' I answered apathetically.

' Dear | The young brute !' said the wait-ing-woman, indignantly. ' I'll call Mrs. Abbott, and show her this moment !'

' No, don't,' I implored, catching her dress; ' don't tell her anything about it. Do let me lie down, Parks.'

Parks soliloquised half a moment ; then her rapid fingers returned to my strings and buttons, and thus her indignant murmurings explained her compliance with my request :

' Well | I may almost as well—for if I do go and bring her, that young fellow is safe to have some fine story on his tongue-tip, to put himself all right with, and make you out all in the wrong. Mrs. Abbott always believes what he likes to say, too. I can't make it out | If he was anybody else, she'd see through him in a minute, but, somehow, *he's* found out how to throw dust in her eyes. There | get into bed, dear. Does

that pain you ? I'll fetch some of Mrs.
Abbott's toilet vinegar, and put it on for
you.'

Partly this speech, which I had not forgotten, partly the conviction that no torture
could be being carried on while the tormentor was away, and partly the fact that I
should have perforce to tell my tale like a
sneak, behind the back of him I accused, had
already weakened the strength of my charge.
Mrs. Abbott's lecture, under the circum
stances, was a sort of carrying the war into
the enemy's country. This wounded my
pride, and Marshall was safe from even my
accusations.

'Henrietta,' began my aunt, 'I don't intend to scold you, my dear, because I think
this illness will in itself be sufficient punish-
ment; but I must not let the matter pass
over without warning you against giving way
to such ungovernable temper. If you rush

into such passions, and make yourself ill
about such mere trifles——'

'He killed my dear little Crisp!' I interrupted. 'It wasn't a trifle!'

'You are sorry to lose your dog, no doubt,'
agreed my aunt, 'but you should have shown
moderation about even your grief for an
animal. But what I am blaming you for is
the violent rage against your brother in
which you indulged, so that you even would
not say "Good-bye" to him, when he had
only done what was absolutely necessary, and
for every one's safety.'

'Why did he say he did it, aunt?'

'Your brother's eyes are more experienced
than yours,' went on Mrs. Marshall, pursuing
the track towards the revelation of Marshall's
story. 'A little girl like you cannot be supposed to know much. Symptoms which you
cannot see tell a very certain tale to him.
He says that your dog had *every* symptom of

hydrophobia, and that it was a mercy that he had not bitten some one before then. There, now, let us say no more about it.'

And we did not say any more about it.

That so stupendous a falsehood should have been conceived in my brother's brain was so alarming a fact that I was content to be silent upon it. A bitter sense of injustice filled my soul. I had a conviction that if I told the whole of my tale this injustice would be intensified by precisely the amount of the wrong I had suffered. No doubt, Marshall had prepared the whole ground for himself in his aunt's mind. Feeling silently certain that my aunt would either disbelieve or disregard my story if she heard it, I shrunk from inflicting upon myself the extra pain of knowing that she absolutely *had* so disbelieved and disregarded. There is a mighty difference between a proved and an unproved mental certainty. In short, my pride dreaded a violent blow; and I perceived no sufficient reason for subjecting it to the danger, for the childish mind has no appreciation of fulfilling a public duty by acting as informer. So I suffered in silence, and said never a word to shake Marshall's position in the opinion of Mrs. Abbott.

Two months passed rapidly away. Mrs. Marshall worked, no doubt, a very distinct alteration in my habits and manners. She kept me with her constantly, and twenty times a day something in my manners, or some form of speech, were stigmatised by her as 'boyish and unladylike.' By degrees, I suppose, I improved, for one day, shortly before Christmas, my aunt asked me, did I know that I was now much more like other girls? and added that she thought I might begin the new year by going to school.

School had no terrors to my uninitiated mind; and though I had come to like Mrs.

Marshall in these two months, it was only in a sedate quiet way—a liking which could be very content to leave the daily presence of its object. On the other hand, I had a strong and pressing reason for wishing to leave Dalestonbury. The dean and my brother were expected home before very long., How I dreaded meeting Marshall again can scarcely be imagined. I would have been glad to go, even had I anticipated being unhappy at school, simply that I might avoid the presence of my brother.

It was, therefore, with satisfaction that I received my aunt's intimation a little while later, that she had selected a school for me ; that said school re-opened on the 15th of January, and that she herself would take me there, and commit me to the hands of my governess.

That she communicated her decision to my

father I learnt by the next little letter which
I had from my dear Willie. His untidy
affectionate notes were very precious to receive. Every little detail about my pets com-
mitted to his charge, the tiniest scrap of
home news, was very sweet to my palate.
At the end of one of his delightful little
scrawls, which came a few days after my
aunt had told me the date fixed for the com-
mencement of my school life, Willie informed
me that he was to go to Rugby, his four
teenth birthday having arrived, a little time
after I should have gone to my school; and
we mutually grieved that we were not to be
at Rugby together. I did not know then, as
I afterwards learnt, that my father never expressed an opinion upon, never even noticed,
Mrs. Marshall's communication to him of the
steps she proposed taking for my education.
He only recognised my existence by the very
practical method of continuing to transfer

from his own account to my uncle's, at their several bankers', the two hundred pounds annually which he had before supplied for my elder brother's expenses. At home, I learned from my brothers, he mentioned my name rarely, and then only as though speaking of one of his absent boys.

The school which my aunt had selected for me was at one of the most exclusive of the north-eastern watering-places. It was large, expensive, and celebrated for its wonderfully mingled solid and fashionable teaching. In the selection of my school, Mrs. Marshall displayed the sound judgment which was ordinarily her characteristic.

Her final advice was delivered to me just before her departure, when we had had an interview with Mrs. Worthington, the school's principal, in a drawing-room with a painfully sombre carpet, and containing a piano with a painfully brilliant silking, on top of

which stood a green obelisk that turned out
to be called a metronome : containing chairs,
somewhat ancient, with cross-looking twisted
legs ; and having a new paper on the wall, the
scent of whose paste hung about, and whose
colours matched neither carpet's, nor piano's,
nor chair's colour. Not the principal's drawing-
room, by any means ; but the room used by the
dancing-mistress to teach the pupils how to
enter and depart through a door, and how to
pilot themselves with grace among a confusion
of chairs, and the room where the pupils
received their occasional visitors ; for both
which purposes it was fittingly a room
wherein was not any furniture in plenty,
save and except only looking-glasses—reflec-
tors which served alike to show the young
ladies their own defects in deportment in
dancing-mistress moments, and to destroy all
feeling of privacy, and consequently all readiness of private speech, in visitors' moments.

My aunt spoke, and across her words broke the melodious notes of three other pianos, each playing its individual tune :

' Henrietta, darling, make up your mind to be comfortable here ; learn how to behave, above all things ; make very few intimate friends ; forget all about anatomy ; and don't squander your money foolishly.'

CHAPTER VI.

I AM not going to write a story of my school-
life. I think it necessary to give this warning at once ; because if I do not, I stand a
very fair chance of having my volume closed
at this point, and carried back to the circu-
lating library, with the remark with which a
lady, who had the most infinitesimal portion
of brain that a human cranium can exist over,
once returned to me Grace Greenwood's
charming ' Recollections,' which I had lent to
her :

' I want something more *mature!*'

And yet, IF it be true that genius is but
originality, and IF I desired to make good a

claim to genius, I *would* write a novel of school-girl life. Mr. Thackeray, in the preface to 'Pendennis,' says that no English writer, since Fielding, has dared to truthfully depict the life of a young man. Who has dared, or will dare, to tell the still more unknown story of the thoughts, words, and ways of a hundred and fifty girls gathered together?

Witty George Augustus Sala has declared the futility of a man's essaying the task. The clerical president may guess, the visiting physician must know, something of the inner life of these temples of fashionable learning. But can even they give the reverse of the picture which sweet Mrs. Hemans saw when she glanced into a girls' schoolroom? Let it not be feared that I will attempt to do so.

A little of the detail of my school-life belongs to my tale, and must be told in consequence.

For a fortnight after my arrival at school, there was a good deal of confusion. More of the pupils came every day, and the whole work of the school was very irregularly done. I was handed about from class to class, and found myself in a state of great uncertainty as to whether I liked or disliked school. Natu-rally proud and haughty, I had scarcely spoken to one of the girls with whom I ate and walked; certainly, had not made the slightest approach to friendship with any-one.

By the end of this time, however, the school began to get into order. Mrs. Worth-ington received the report of her various subordinates on each new pupil, and we were now instructed which teacher we were to be under in the different subjects.

In music, needlework, and various other minor graces, I had to submit to go to be taught in company with girls much younger than myself; but in the English class for which I was found fitted, my fellow-pupils were, without exception, my seniors. It was amongst these girls, however, that I must expect to find my companions.

The position in the English class—that is to say, in every subject for which there was not a special outdoor professor — determined the general rank in the establishment. The co-pupils of one English teacher sat together at the table which she headed in the dining-room, and slept under her general supervision, in companies of six in each large bedroom.

For the first two weeks I had slept alone in a small room opening into one occupied by the three articled pupils; but when Mrs. Worthington called my name to join Miss Morris's English class, I was removed also to Miss Morris's table, and to one of her bed-rooms.

Mrs. Worthington, having separated the

young ladies who were judged worthy of becoming Miss Morris's pupils, led them herself to their new teacher's class-room, where her old scholars were already gathered. The principal opened the door, and, as we filed in, ceremonially introduced each of us to our teacher, by name. Then she immediately departed, and we were bidden by Miss Morris to sit all together at the foot of the class until we had 'earned better places.'

I had not seen Miss Morris before; she had only returned to her duties on the previous Saturday. She was henceforth to be a very considerable person in my life, and I therefore surveyed her with much interest, and a little anxiety.

Externally, the result was entirely satisfactory. Miss Morris was rather short, and slight. Her features were very clearly and sharply defined, without the least appearance of being pinched. Her hair was fair; and the noticeable expression of her eyes was their perfect calm. If Miss Morris had been an indolent member of the *grande monde*, I suppose that her eyes would have been either weary or scornful in their silent expressiveness; as she was instead a troubled and energetic worker for her daily bread, their still, keen clearness conveyed only the idea of perfect calm.

The commencing lesson of this day happened to be English history. The pupils ought all to have read over in their books the evening before that portion which was to form the subject of the morning lesson. Now, therefore, our books were not to be opened; instead of that, the teacher sitting in her place in our midst, having her book open, but never glancing at it, gave us, in clear concise language, and with an impressiveness that made inattention impossible, a *résumé* of the subject on which the class was then engaged.

Then she began to question her pupils, commencing at the head.

When a girl could not answer the question she was asked, she had not to exchange her position in the class for that of the one who did reply to it, however low down it might be, but simply went into the place of the one next beneath herself. By this means, I know that complete justice was done. A temporary failure of memory never condemned a girl to a position very inferior to that which she really merited; while, at the same time, a girl who scarcely ever lost a place rose slowly, but surely, to her proper position at or near the head of the class. This was a peculiar arrangement of Miss Morris's own. I learned that it did not obtain in any other English class.

Very quickly when this latter part of the lesson began, a peculiarity became apparent to me. Just what there was uncommon, I did not discover for a considerable time; but as this is to be the only chapter devoted to my school-life, and as my teacher was so remarkable a woman, and unquestionably had so great an influence in the formation of my character that I cannot resist giving at least an outline sketch of her strong individuality, I will write here what I did not know for some time later.

It was a rule of the school that no practical enforcement of her laws should be permitted to any teacher. Even the infliction of a short additional task for misbehaviour might not be given. Every fault, if the teacher desired it noticed, must be reported to the principal, and was punished or forgiven at her discretion.

I know that many of the scholars were 'received into the establishment to fill a few vacancies on greatly reduced terms,' as the prospectus put it; I know also that the friends of the richer pupils frequently made presents to the principal ; nevertheless, I by no means assert that any other motive than a wish to secure a certainty of justice dictated the rule I have mentioned.

But its existence, and the decision with which Mrs. Worthington enforced it, dismissing instantly any teacher infringing it, were very unpleasant and inconvenient facts to those much-tried ladies. Miss Morris alone, of all the teachers under whom I was from the beginning to the end of my stay there, seemed competent to rule on these conditions without either difficulty to herself or demoralisation to her class.

Her weapon was satire ; keen and stinging as a whip of fine cords. Always so delicate and refined that its strength was often not instantly perceptible, but only brought a sudden flush of understanding to its victim's cheek when repeated by memory ; yet so

keen, and often so pointed, that I never
knew a girl whose stupidity and self-compla-
cency it could not finally succeed in piercing.
Her voice had a particularly clear calm tone
in saying these severe things, which was to
her irony precisely what the steely shine is to
the surgeon's lancet—the cold glitter drawing the attention of a watcher to the effect of
the cut.

In addition to this, she had a wonderful
power of winning the attachment of those
who were often with her. I have mentioned
that all her other pupils were considerably
my seniors. The girls—almost young women
—who thus surrounded her were just capable
of appreciating her mental excellences.

The devotion which they, with very few
exceptions, poured upon her was one of the
most singular things I have ever known.
The prouder, the more reserved, and the
more intellectual the nature of a girl, the

more firmly fixed became the influence of
Miss Morris over her; and the long conversa-
tions which the teacher would hold with the
pupils out of school hours, so far from prov-
ing that familiarity breeds contempt, aided
and ensured earnest attention and watchful
eagerness to please from the girls in
class.

That which I felt existing in her circle on
this morning, and which I knew had not
been present in any one of the many other
classes in which I had been temporarily
placed during the preceding fortnight, was
the result of these two individualisms of the
teacher. Her old pupils were so uncommonly
anxious to obtain her praise ; a word of approval, given in the low earnest tone which
marked it out from her satirical commendation,
seemed to confer so much pleasure, and there
was such a total absence of what I should at
the time have termed 'bullying,' that the

difference could not fail to be felt by the most careless school-girl.

The first three of the class answered with perfect correctness the questions put to them. The third was especially long and difficult.

' Evidently you have not lost your memory in the vacation,' said the teacher, with a very sweet smile moving her lips; ' but Miss Grey and Miss Andrews do not intend you to conquer them easily, you see.'

Which few words brought a gratified look to the faces of all three for the remainder of the lesson.

The questions passed down the class with varying results in individual cases, till at length the teacher reached the last of the old pupils. This was a slight girl, with a profusion of hair of an undecided pale tint, and a peculiar way of glancing through her downcast lashes. Miss Morris addressed her as ' Miss Manseargh,' and put to her a question upon a point which had been especially dwelt upon in her address. But the girl stood dumb.

' The answer is not written on the floor, Miss Manseargh,' said the teacher presently ; ' if you do not know, be good enough to look toward me, and tell me so.'

Without obeying the request to lift her eyes, Miss Manseargh answered in passionless tones, ' I do not know, Miss Morris.'

The next girl—the first of the new ones— replied correctly to this question, and took the higher place. Instead of passing over Miss Manseargh, as I knew she had done over those who had before failed to answer a question, Miss Morris immediately put to her a second query. For sole reply, the girl folded her hands and looked upon them.

' Miss Manseargh's soul has mounted from her boots to her finger-nails,' said Miss Morris in her coldest tones ; ' we shall possibly get it to her brain presently. Can the next young lady give her this answer ?'

The next young lady could, and did, and forthwith took the higher place. Miss Morris instantly put a third question to the unfortunate Miss Manseargh. She still stood immovably silent. The scene was beginning to impress me very much. It was evidently no new contest. And, young as I was, the contrast between the fiery wrath held down behind the teacher's calm eyes and clear voice, and the cool impassiveness of the scholar, presented itself to me in full force.

Another place was ceded by Miss Manseargh.

'Of course, I am only complying with your wishes in giving you these opportunities of quickly reaching your old place,' said Miss Morris, as she put to the silent student yet another question.

The girl was now standing next to me. The question was simply the date of a great battle, which had been familiar to me for years. Partly for her sake, partly for our teacher's, I whispered the words into her ear. Still she did not speak.

'You may happen to discover that you need all the abilities you possess to keep your own place, Miss Abbott,' said Miss Morris's voice (and I did not find out the sting in the sentence for a long time). 'However,' she added, 'as you have answered the question, you can take the place.'

In a little time more, Miss Manseargh had reached the foot of the class. There she stayed for the rest of the time, never taking a place. But every now and then Miss Morris's attention seemed to turn itself to her, and elicit a sharp remark. For example, in rebuke to a girl who had lost several places, Miss Morris said,—

'You will be next the bottom presently, Miss Dyer. You seem to intend to be next to the worst in my class!' The accent conveyed the deepest meaning of the sentence to the very worst, who would always foot the list.

At twelve o'clock the classes ceased for a time, and an hour's vacation came before dinner. I went out into the garden, and sat down upon one of its seats to re-read Willie's last letter. It had come the day before, accompanied by a parcel containing a book. Willie wrote :

'Father has bought you and me the same new year's present. It is quite a new book, and the master had it bound in leather on purpose for us. As you are going to get out of that Deanery, I hope you will not have it taken away from you. Let us agree to read it, and see which of us gets on farthest against we meet. I told the master your anatomy was taken away, but he did not speak.'

The book was a standard work on physiology. I had determined to keep it in the seclusion of my trunk, and fulfil Willie's request to read it only when I could do so privately. I have the book at this day. It was my father's last gift of its kind to me. I read it and studied it a great deal at intervals, partly because it was my only medical work, and really interested me, partly to be able to tell Willie, when I should see him next, that I had mastered it.

As I finished reading over his letter—colloquial and inelegant, but so very precious—I discovered that some one had sat down on the seat during my abstraction. I looked at that some one, and saw it was Miss Manseargh. She was quietly regarding me through her lashes, and made some slight remark, nothing disconcerted, when I detected her in the act.

Her words, whatever they were, opened a conversation. She drew me into a talk, and presently we were chatting quite like old acquaintances.

At last we got into the school-room.

'Don't you like Miss Morris?' I asked, remembering the morning's scene.

'No! I detest her,' said my companion, using energetic words, but speaking quite without energy.

'What is that for? and why didn't you answer any questions?' I asked, infringing etiquette with impunity, in the absence of my pastors and masters.

'She detests me, too,' said my new friend, directing a most effective and plaintive glance up at me through her lashes. 'I am obliged to give her a good deal of trouble. But I cannot help it'—a sigh, and the interesting air of a little penitent—'I would give anything to prevent worrying her so much.'

'Why,' said I, with unsophisticated bluntness, 'you could surely have answered one of
all those questions—at least, if you had
learned your lesson ?'

'She would put me down to the foot of
the class somehow or other in time,' said
Miss Manseargh pensively. 'She wants me
there, and I may as well go at once ! But I
do not mean that at all.'

'What is it, then ?' I inquired. There
was something very pretty in the glances of
her grey eyes through her dark lashes. My
eyes were getting fascinated by them ; I was
learning to watch for them, to desire to draw
them out. Her undecided-coloured hair, too,
was arranged in a very unusual manner, that
was interesting to look at. Away from
Miss Morris, in the presence of this girl,
my opinion of the teacher became uncertain.

'I sleep in her bed,' said Miss Manseargh,

'and she has to have my wrist tied to hers with a strap.'

'Jupiter!' said I, astonishment restoring one of the expressions which my aunt had carefully weeded out of my vocabulary. 'What on earth *is* that for ?'

'I walk in my sleep !—that is to say, I might do. I have done a few times, and they are afraid that I might get into some danger in my sleep. I am in Miss Morris's room, and, of course, she has to take the trouble. But she dislikes me very much because of it.'

'What a shame !' said I, indignantly, swallowing the whole story. 'Why don't you sleep with one of the girls instead ?'

'None of them would take so much trouble for me,' she replied, with another of her glances. 'They would very likely be frightened.'

'*I* shouldn't be frightened,' I said haughtily.

'Oh, would you,' with half indifferent rapture, 'would you take the trouble? Do you know, I thought you and I would be great friends. I thought so before I spoke to you. And,' with tones of tenderness, ' I want some one to be fond of me.'

After a little more talk, in the course of which I learnt that my new acquaintance was named Helen, that she was twelve years old, and that her father was not alive, I consented to go to Mrs. Worthington and ask her permission to become night-keeper of Miss Manseargh.

With considerable trepidation I followed the directions of my new friend to the door of Mrs. Worthington's private apartments. That lady had evidently forgotten me, but found out my name, and remembering my identity, became gracious to me.

' I should not object, dear,' she said, ' but I cannot authorise it. The responsibility lies

upon Miss Morris, your teacher. If you ask
her, you may tell her that I gave my permission, so far as I interfere with such arrangements.'

I went back to Helen Manseargh and
reported progress. She appeared tolerably
satisfied, and told me that she knew which
bed Miss Morris had assigned me, and that
I had at present no bedfellow, and that I
should ask permission to undertake the
charge when my bed was pointed out to me
in the evening. When that time came, and
Miss Morris led her new pupils to the rooms
under her superintendence, I, in due course,
preferred my request.

Miss Morris stopped, and looked scru-
tinisingly at me; then turned.

' Of course, Miss Manseargh, you have
asked Miss Abbott to undertake this?'

' Yes, Miss Morris,' said Helen indif-
ferently; ' but she will not think it very

great trouble.' There was nothing meaning,
nothing sarcastic, in her tones. Even if Miss
Morris had been likely to openly resent a
speech such as this, she would not have been
able to do so.

'You must not permit yourself to be de-
ceived or imposed upon, dear Miss Abbott,'
said my teacher, fixing her eyes upon me
with a very sweet and tender expression.
'But as your bed is in my room, and I sleep
very lightly, I think this will be perfectly
safe ; you may do so, if you please.'

My heart sank a little ; but I thanked her
very earnestly, more for the kindness of her
tones than for the favour.

However, Helen Manscargh and I slept
thenceforward in one bed ; and I, not of a
temperament to make many friends, gradually
came to lavish all my immediate thoughts
and affection upon her. Not blindly, by any
means. Helen depended upon me, although

she was two years my senior. I quarrelled
for her, did all her work for her that was
possible, and helped her and stirred her up
to her own studies. I was repaid by her
glances, by her thanks, by her mere de-
pendence upon me. Nevertheless, I knew—
I felt at first, and in a few years became
analytically conscious—that she was very
weak, very selfish, very cold-hearted. Yet
I loved her with a strong, firm affection, and
only saw her faults to shield her from their
consequences.

Very soon I found how she had misrepre-
sented Miss Morris to me. Miss Morris disliked Helen, undoubtedly; probably her fine
moral sense detected the girl's failings from
the first, while I was bound in affection
before I discovered them. But it is to me
at this day something of a psychological
puzzle how I could at one and the same time
admire Miss Morris with reverent appre-

ciation, and give so warm and protecting an affection to Helen Manseargh, who was so totally incapable of understanding either her teacher or me.

Under the influence of a fashionable school, of this companion, and this teacher and friend, the next seven years of my life passed without any great events.

CHAPTER VII.

It is seven years since Helen Manseargh and I, Henrietta Abbott, met, for the first time, in the class-room downstairs. Time has built up these seven years by moments ; and in like manner he increases the stature and development of the children of men. We who stand in this upper room of Athena House are no longer the children who answered seven years ago in its class-rooms to the same names as we do now; but young women, albeit only school-girls still.

There are no seven years of so great development, so complete change, as those which separate twelve from twenty. These

wonderful years! How they round the
arms, define the bust, clear out the features,
and work ·a revolution in thoughts, feelings,
and desires! A portion of this time has
passed over our heads, and that which was
only foreshadowed and predicted by child-
hood is now fixed and certain for evermore—
a character.

All through these seven years, Helen
Manseargh and I had remained fast friends;
had slept in each other's arms, and had held
as one common stock our confidences, our
stores, and our raiment. I knew that this
arrangement was, so far as material be-
longings went, highly advantageous to
Helen. My adornments and my purse,
always placed freely at her service, far ex-
ceeded hers in value and quantity. But I
rejoiced in my superior wealth only because
it gave me the happiness of being instru-
mental in her pleasure. When I spent an

evening in altering the disposition of the trimming on one of my costly hats, that the teachers might not recognise it as mine when it should adorn Helen's head at church, or when I gave her some present, expensive by comparison with my resources, I was far more than repaid by a slight embrace, enthusiastic for her, by a look from her eyes— sleepy, but thrilling—up through her eyelashes, and by being told in her low tones, with a dash of melancholy in them, that I was the dearest thing in the world.

Helen was poor. She had acknowledged this to me, with her peculiar proud, sorrowful humility, very soon. But she took care to impress upon me also that the poverty of her mother was owing entirely to her father's misfortunes, and the wickedness of those he had trusted. Her family was old. Its private history wound back until it reached a monarch who lived and reigned over an Irish

province in days of antiquity. Some of
Helen's relatives were rich, too. It was a
bequest from one of them, her godmother,
that paid for her expensive education.

She had been about to leave school in ordinary course more than a year before, when she
reached her eighteenth birthday. I felt dreadfully unhappy at the thought of losing her daily
companionship ; and Helen had mentioned
to me how her mother grieved that it would
be impossible for her to enter the society to
which her birth should admit her. Putting
these facts together, I appealed movingly to
my aunt Marshall. Helen passed the greater
part of the vacation preceding the one when
she should have left school at the Deanery
with me. She succeeded in making a very
good impression on Mrs. Marshall. My
aunt, by cautious inquiries, satisfied herself
of the relationship between Mrs. Francis
Manseargh and the Mansearghs of County

Kerry and County Cork, the Burkes of Kerry, and a dozen others ; all grand people enough, of high position, but whose relationship to my poor Helen would never be of any more advantage to her than the mere connection implied. This important point of identity certain, my aunt's benevolence came into full play. When Helen went home to her mother, who lived, in what style I knew not, at a little Kentish watering-place, called Rusport, she carried with her a very ceremonious letter from Mrs. Marshall Abbott to Mrs. Francis Manseargh, which said, in substance, that if Helen were permitted to remain with me at school for about a year and a half longer, my aunt would then invite her on a visit, and introduce her into society at the same time as I appeared. The answer came in an envelope sealed with the Manseargh crest, very large sized, and written on the thickest of cream-coloured paper. It

9—2

was somewhat lengthy, and gushing—'cha-
racteristically national,' my aunt said, a little
cruelly. It accepted the offer gratefully.
The writer's relatives—here followed a long
list of names, headed by an Irish earl's, who
was about a seventh cousin—would all be
pleased to receive in their houses Francis
Manseargh's daughter, but none of them
were prepared to chaperone her, and as the
writer's own circumstances prevented her
from doing so herself, she accepted Mrs.
Marshall Abbott's most generous offer with
the deepest gratitude of a fond mother.

There was a great deal more than this in
it ; numberless allusions to the author's own
family, and several paragraphs bemoaning
her hard fate in being excluded by fortune
from the position to which she was born.
Altogether, the letter seemed to give my
aunt an amused notion of the individuality
of Helen's mother. However, her birth, as

well as her marriage, gave her an unexceptionable title to position, and democracy has not yet shaken one atom the aristocratic power of mere birth.

So Helen and I had stayed on together at Athena House, continuing to mount from class to class, and to change from room to room, in company. For only about six months after our first meeting had we continued to fasten one another's wrists to a long strap when we were going to bed. Helen had only been known to walk in her sleep four or five times, each occasion being when she was in some trouble, and concurrently occupying a strange room. She had done so last immediately after her father died, when she first came to school; but we soon decided that there was no danger of its recurrence; and, after about six months of intimacy, we appealed against our restriction to the head authorities, and were freed therefrom on Miss

Morris's responsibility. Helen had never shown any disposition to sleep-walking since that time, and we had all but forgotten that ever she had done so.

On this particular evening, when our friendship was of seven years' growth, Helen and I were in an upper room of Mrs. Worthington's establishment, preparing for dissipation—of the very mildest character, however.

It was the thirteenth of June, and the day of "breaking-up" for the midsummer vacation. A ticketed public distribution of half-yearly prizes by the Lord Bishop of the Diocese had taken place in the morning. In the evening there was a *soirée*, to which the elder pupils were invited to meet a select company of neighbouring respectabilities, all of mature age. Dissipation of the milk-and-waterish type ; a very model of recreative tameness, but dissipation nevertheless.

' Helen, my child,' I said, discontentedly,

after manipulating vainly for several moments, ' it's no use ; pearls will not look well with your plaits, however I twist them.'

Helen took the candle in her hand, and put her face close to the glass, bending her head from side to side to get a better view.

' I haven't light enough,' she proclaimed. ' Do step across and borrow Kitty Fuller's candle for a moment.'

' She'll be dressing herself ; she won't lend it to me.'

' Well, but whose else could I have ? And I must see myself, Harry. Go and ask her, there's a darling ! Coax her, you know !'

Reluctantly I stepped across the passage, and went in at the opposite door. A girl in white bodice and petticoat sat stitching bugles on to a band, her needle flying in a way that proclaimed her haste.

' Kitty,' said I, ' lend me your candle for two minutes, there's a sweet creature.'

'Can't—no time—bring your's here ;'—not raising her head from her work.

' It isn't for me alone ; — just one minute.'

'Oh! you are dressing your dolly, are you? Let dolly go with one hair out of place, for once in the way.'

' Kitty,' pleadingly, 'don't tease ! Just one half second.'

' I tell you, you pay a great deal too much attention to that baby of yours. I would lend you the candle for yourself; but if Helen Manseargh wants to contemplate her own beauty while you act her waiting-maid, she must come over here (and then I shall watch the fun)'—the last words added in a stage ' aside' as I turned away.

' Helen,' I said, re-entering our room, 'you shouldn't send me to Kitty Fuller; she is safe to say something aggravating.'

'Hateful thing,' said Helen, placidly. 'Why,

you haven't brought the candle after all !' she
added in surprised tones.

· ' She says that if you want it, you must go
over there.'

' Oh ! I can't do that ; can I ? '

' No, of course not.'

' What *is* to be done then, Harry dear ? '
in tones expressive of the most plaintive
sorrow ; tones that moved my fond heart.

' I'll steal down to the kitchen and bribe
cookey !' I exclaimed, boldly, after a moment's
hesitation.

My mistress had the grace to demur in the
following effective manner.

' You dearest ! but I don't want you to
get into a bother ; Mrs. Worthington would
be very cross.'

' I don't suppose anyone would meet me ;
they're all dressing.'

' It is giving you *so* much trouble ; but,
really, I can't see myself by this light ; and

you will have to put on your dark dress again;
but, then, if you get some, you will be able to
see better for yourself, won't you, dear ?'

I was resignedly putting on again my thick
skirt, and as my generous, unselfish beloved
finished this speech, I opened the door quietly
and went away down the stairs.   I have mentioned the incident because it was thoroughly
characteristic, a typical incident of our position and our daily lives.   It was no light
yoke under which I laboured ; no small burden that my own freewill bound upon my
shoulders.   In proud submission I served her
and did her will in all small things.   At the
same time I was, and we both knew that I
was, her superior, mentally and morally.   On
the rare occasions on which I asserted my
judgment against hers, she yielded at discretion, with just such murmurings as a spoilt
child might have uttered.   But in every-day
matters the power was hers, and ruthlessly

she used it. If Helen Manseargh retain her fascination until she shall count fifty years, I am certain that she never can have a lover more devoted to her service, more subservient to her slightest wish, than I, the lover of her school days.

I accomplished my journey to the lower regions in safety, and effected an exchange between a piece of silver from my purse, and a scrap of candle. By aid of the double illumination, Helen inspected herself to her own satisfaction, and coincided with my opinion that pearls would not do. They took away all the charm of her strange, undecidedly shaded hair, and themselves looked dusky and dirty beside it. So I twined some artificial leaves in her plaits, and hung a rosebud above her ear. When her attiring was quite complete, she condescended to say I was the best, and—I should be late if I didn't be quick!

I took the rejected string of pearls—they belonged to me, by the way—and twisted them around my own curls, to keep them away from my face. The pure white beads harmonised well with my dark hair, and gained in whiteness by their setting.

'I had these pearls in my hair the last time I saw Willie,' I said, smiling at myself; 'it was at Dalestonbury, last year, and I remember it because he said he liked the effect so much.'

'How fond you are of Willie !' said Helen, with the tinge of a sneer in her voice. 'I believe you love Willie a great deal better than you do me, Harry.'

'Don't talk nonsense, Helen,' I advised; 'I'm very fond of you both. I haven't any need to remember you when you are always with me. I see dear Willie so seldom.'

'Will you see him this vacation ?' asked

Helen, with a little more interest than a question of hers usually displayed.

'I am rather afraid not,' I replied, putting in an earring; 'that letter I had this morning was from him—you can look at it, if you are not too lazy to get it out of my pocket,' interrupting myself.

'But I am.' Helen had bestowed herself upon one of our chairs, with due regard to her muslin, and had elevated her feet upon the other to watch my dressing. 'What did he say?'

'He has just had an honour bestowed upon him. One of the physicians to the hospital has just opened a small dispensary, and has given the charge of it to him—the charge of one branch, that is.'

'Really? Is that remarkable?'

'Oh, it is a great honour, while he is still a student in his second year.'

'Rather a tiresome honour, I should say,'

remarks Indolence, from her extemporised couch.

'He doesn't think so, I can tell you. But the fact is, he is not a student like most young men are—just picking up the rudiments of the study. He learnt *them* with me when he was a boy of twelve, sitting in the big arm-chair with me beside him at Apsland. The seed that was planted then is growing now. And he had a real love for the study, just like I had, and has kept it up.'

'He has had special opportunities, this paragon of brothers, has he not?'

'Oh yes; he has been studying with our uncle Henry all the time he has been reading for that dreadful London University examination. And he passed that exam.—the arts, you know—so brilliantly that I dare say his professors have always kept him in view.'

'Come here, and let me tie your velvet.' Then, when I was kneeling on the ground before her, 'He seems to empty his heart to you, Harry. I suppose he will tell you all his secrets, up to his falling in love.'

'And he will then!'

'Ah! *stupide.* You have jerked that artistic bow untied in my fingers. How do you know that he will?'

'I am as certain of that, my dear child, as I am of my name.'

'Tiresome thing! there was no need to twist round like that to make your speech. Go with your bow anyhow, if you *can't* curb your energy for one moment. But, Harry, you sent him those eternal slippers on his twenty-first birthday, a week or two back, didn't you?'

'Yes.' I groaned as I remembered the elaborate pattern, every stitch of which sentiment had caused me to put in with my own fingers.

'You don't suppose that he has got to that

mature time of life without ever falling in love, do you?'

'Where is the shoe-horn for my slippers, Helen?'

'In the corner, behind you, Harry. Do you seriously believe a man has got to twenty-one years of age without falling in love? Don't put me off with shoe-horns, darling.'

I answered, struggling with obstinate white kid, 'Willie has, at all events, my child. Some-how or other, we seem not to be a falling-in-love family. Why, five, or even six, of my brothers are old enough for that sort of thing, and only Marshall has married; Lynton is actually getting on for thirty, and Aunt Henry has been helping Aunt Marshall to find him a wife for the last ten years, I believe. The heir of Apsland might have choice enough, I suppose; but he isn't even engaged yet. Here is your handkerchief, dear.'

'Thanks, darling. What is the time?'

'A quarter past eight. I am ready now. We must go downstairs.'

This Helen prepared to do by requesting me to find the buttonhook out of her top drawer, and, like a sweetest, to fasten her glove therewith; and to tell her was her hair quite smooth; and, like a benevolent darling, to lift the chair from under her feet; after which we went down to the drawing-room arm-in-arm.

CHAPTER VIII.

A ROOM which was a blaze of light, a furnace of heat, a Babel of confusion, was the drawing-room to which we wended our way. Mrs. Worthington, arrayed in all her glory, was the first individualisable person. She was posted just inside the door, and her countenance when she beheld us assumed a peculiar mixture of the expression of a hostess receiving guests, and a governess-principal scrutinising the practical result of her deportment teacher's instructions. Her address, too, was a sort of a made dish of a reception speech.

'Good evening, young ladies! Good evening,

my dear Miss Abbott! I am glad you are down punctually. I hope you will find some-one you know ; if not, let me introduce you to some ladies. We will beg you to favour us with some music presently. Professor Grigoni has reported that you sing some very good duets. Come this way!' all deli-vered, sweetly smiling, benignantly encou-raging.

'This way' was to the shrine of an old lady with a painfully-yellow dress and very deaf ears. She was invited on the score of a juvenile granddaughter, of very low scholastic standing, and of whom neither Helen nor I had ever heard.

'Lady Smith, will you permit me the honour ?' bawled Mrs. Worthington, bending from her stately height to the ear of the yellow dame. 'Miss Abbott, Miss Man-seargh—two of my favourite pupils in the upper class.'

Lady Smith was cruelly thus aroused from a reverie. She fumbled awhile for her glasses, fixed them on her nose, and at last examined us severally. Her ladyship was seated on a couch, one-sixth of which was covered by her tiny person, five-sixths of which were monopolised by her flowing yellow robes. The robes made no movement to give us room. But my lady prepared to cross-examine us standing up before her, as erst, perchance, the deceased alderman, her husband, had cross-examined other culprits.

' *What* is your name, my dear?' scrutinising me through her glasses—said glasses having a peculiar effect in hiding entirely the lids and lashes of the eye, and presenting to me the appearance of an eyeball framed in gold.

'Abbott, madam,' I answered from the elevation of my tallness and in my natural voice.

' Oh, a great deal louder, please !' remarked

Lady Smith with unblinking gaze, and in the tone of one who offers an innocent observation.

I bent down as near to her as I could without losing my balance, and repeated my name as loudly as modesty would permit me.

' Yes,' said the yellow lady peacefully. ' Any relation to Alderman Parrot, my dear ?'

I shook my head, as the most available way of vigorously repudiating this relationship.

' Do you belong to this neighbourhood, Miss Parrot ?' went on my catechist.

' No, madam ;' conveyed as before.

' Where, then?' queried the yellow dowager.

Naturally disinclined to proclaim the name of my home on this housetop, I became busy with the fastening of my glove, and did not hear the question.

My lady deliberately took off her gold-

rimmed spectacles, and gently tapped my
hand to draw my attention ; then repeated,
' Where of ?'

Exasperated, I replied, feeling that I was
telling the entire room ;—of course I wasn't,
there was so much noise, but I felt so.   ' Of
Abbey Castle, Devonshire, my lady.'

But, alas ! my lady heard not only with
her ears.   Slowly she resumed her spectacles,
and brought her gaze to bear upon me, then
repeated, " Where of ?' and waited for the
answer.

I, flushed, was constrained to repeat the
information.

' Miss Parrot, of Abbey Castle, Devonshire
—yes,' agreed our yellow examiner.   ' And
your name, my dear ?' turning to Helen the
fixed, unwinking gaze.

Helen had the advantage of being a great
deal shorter than I, and therefore much
nearer her ladyship's level, and of possessing

a voice which fitted the soprano parts of our duets. But I, who knew by heart every expression of her face, saw thereon the droop of the eyelid and the elevation of the corners of the lips, which I knew betokened extreme dissatisfaction with her task. However, she gave the information without outward and visible sign of anger, and with her lips near the helix of my lady's ear, to whose auditory nerve the sound travelled successfully.

' Yes,' said our yellow cross-examiner, slightly puzzled ; ' German, my dear ?'

' Tell her, Harry !' said Helen to me, with an imploring glance.

' County Kerry, Ireland, Lady Lumley Smith,' said I, complying.

' Oh, Paddy !' said my lady, and giggled, thinking she had been witty.

' What an old idiot,' observed Helen, scornfully, into my ear.

' Never mind, dear,' I said, consolingly,

'What can one expect from a woman dressed in that colour ?—vulgar creature !'

'Do you know my grand-daughter, my dears?' inquired Lady Smith, happily ignorant of these speeches, and incapable of understanding the slight expression of opinion which our well-bred countenances might, under the circumstances, convey.

'What is her name ?' asked I, doubtfully.

'Miss Margaret Smith.'

I looked at Helen, and she returned my glance with one of her characteristic ones of ignorance and indifference combined. I was constrained to reply. 'No, Lady Smith, I think not.'

'Goodness gracious me !' said my lady, with a suddenness of astonishment that was quite startling. Then, after a moment's pause, 'What *do* they teach you here ?'

The conjunction of which remarks so exactly

struck my sense of the comical that I had great difficulty in restraining a laugh. We were fortunately spared replying by the advent of a lady and gentleman who knew Lady Smith, and were waiting for a pause in our conversation to speak to her. She had been stricken dumb with astonishment long enough to afford them the opportunity. And at the very moment, Mrs. Worthington, whose eyes seemed, for this evening, to be in every place, came by with an elderly gentleman, from whose arm she disengaged herself sweetly, and requested him to take us to have some tea. Now, he was French, and delighted in finding victims to whom to pour forth a flood of his native tongue. But the gabbling of his eloquence roamed to no high theme. First the carpet, from whence, by easy transition, to Gobelins tapestry, which work he glorified. Then tea, a beverage of which the French drank much less than the English, which wisdom he glorified. Then cake, a culinary achievement impossible to any but French cooks, whom he glorified.

'Dreadfully slow, isn't it, Harry?' said Helen, having, with the coolness of an experienced *demoiselle de société*, despatched our cavalier for the biscuits from the other end of the *buffet*.

'Awfully aggravating,' I responded, as usual the most energetic of the two. When lo! behind us, having overheard both slangy sentences, our majestic principal, with a gentleman, to whom, after a momentary glance I sprang joyfully. 'Willie!'

I certainly might have proceeded to embrace the dear fellow in the coffee-room, but he, more experienced in polite repression, wisely took both of my hands in his warm clasp, and smiled with all the fondness of his affection in his eyes.

'You shall see your brother alone, before

he goes, Miss Abbott,' said Mrs. Worthington, ' but he and I both think that you had better not just yet. He will be good enough to stay through the evening with you. You will come back into the drawing-room for the present; therefore, Miss Manseargh, perhaps you had better come with me.'

' Oh no, Mrs. Worthington!' I interrupted, ' please let Helen stay with me.'

' Well, for the present. M. Bourgon, will you take me back to the drawing-room?' and our principal kindly carried off our French attendant.

' Darling old Harry !' was my brother's word-of-mouth greeting.

' Dear, dear old fellow !' I responded, and we embraced with our eyes for a moment, then—' Helen !' I exclaimed, taking my hand out of Willie's, ' You and Willie know one another well enough in reality, though there seems to have been a fatality against your meeting one another. I am so glad you see each other at last.' Then, ending as I should have begun, 'Helen, my brother Willie; Miss Manseargh, Willie.'

They looked at each other and bowed, coldly and calmly enough. There was a much greater degree of interest for one another in them than the parties to an introduction commonly have. For my heart was about divided between them, and while my letters to Willie had often been full of Helen, she had read all his letters to me, and had been kept in possession of all his achievements and doings from my lips. But 'Coming events cast their shadows before,' is not a true proverb in every sense. No foreshadowing of the future invested this meeting with the thrilling interest that belonged to it, in that connection.

For the rest of the evening we had what our American fellow-linguists would call a real good time. My brother had the polish

and the experience of two seasons of London
drawing-rooms, to aid his natural powers of
making himself agreeable. Helen arose from
her apathy, and all her peculiar and characteristic variations, which had always been so
charming and fascinating to me—girls though
we both were—came into play. The shifting
shades of her hair, the brief glances through
her long eyelashes, the rising and falling
colour, and the melancholy inflection of her
voice ; all her individual charms, all those
fascinating peculiarities which marked her out
from all other women I ever knew, displayed
themselves in full force. We found a quiet
corner in the drawing-room, and talked of
every possible thing ; we drank lukewarm
tea, and ate stale cake ; and the only young
man in the room leant over our music when
we sang our long-practised duet. A certain
shade of quiet and sobriety hung over Willie
all the time ; but I attributed this to the

weighty responsibilities of a dispensary physician. The explanation of his sudden appearance he refused to give until the end of the evening.

At length the guests began to depart. Mrs. Worthington took her first spare moment to come to my side, and tell me to go down to the visitors' room for ten minutes, to bid goodnight to my brother.

'You remain with me, Miss Manseargh!' was added so peremptorily that we did not question the mandate.

'Harry, darling,' said Willie, putting his arm round me, 'I have some sad news for you. I would not interrupt your enjoyment of the evening to no purpose. I am sorry to have to give it a sad ending.'

'Father?' I said, alarmed by this beginning.

'No. Father is not ill,' he hastened to reassure me. 'No, dearest. But we have

lost a brother. Poor James has died in
Bengal, where you know the ——th was
quartered.'

'Poor boy!' I said, some tears filling my
eyes, and real sorrow my heart. 'You remember him better than I do, no doubt,
Willie; but he is my brother. And so
young! He came between Lynton and
Marshall; and one is twenty-nine, the other
twenty-five. He would be only seven-and-
twenty, Willie?'

'Exactly,' said Willie. 'Now, love, Aunt
Marshall thinks there is a duty falling upon
you, through this, and that is why I am
here. This letter will tell you what she
thinks you have to do.'

I took the black-bordered epistle, and
broke open the envelope. It was written in
my aunt's bold, decided hand, duly headed
by her monogram, opposite the Abbott crest,
engraved above 'Dalestonbury Deanery,

——shire,' in inexplicable Old English letters.
Thus it said :

' My dear Henrietta,

'The sad news has reached us
of the early death of your brother
James. You, who know how affectionate a
father Mr. Abbott is, and how proud and
fond he has always been of his sons, will feel
how great a blow this will be to him. He is
very much isolated from society. Lynton
and Everard are on the Continent ; Willie is
tied to his post : only Marshall is near your
father, and you know that his unfortunate
marriage has placed a coolness between
him and Mr. Abbott. The dean and I
alike feel that your duty and privilege is
to go to your father in this sorrow, and cheer
and comfort him. It is your especial province
to do so, as his only daughter. We would
have deferred your going to see him until

after you had come out, but for this occurrence. Under the circumstances, we all think that you should go to Abbey Castle at once. I must tell you that your father has never seemed to rejoice in your sex, though he has received my report of your progress with interest. You must go, now, and make him thank God for his one daughter. Willie will bring you this letter, and accompany you up to London, from whence some friends of mine will chaperon you as far as Exeter, whence, of course, you drive by post.

' I know your self-reliance and judgment, my dear Henrietta, or perhaps I should hesitate to send you thus alone. But it will be better that no one accompanies you. The housekeeper can provide for you, certainly ; and for your behaviour to your father I must leave you to your own good taste and sense.

' Give my kind regards to Miss Manseargh,

and express to her my great regret that this
sad event must cause the postponement of
her visit to Dalestonbury.

'Be sure you write to me immediately you
get settled at home. Give my love to your
father—our condolences the dean and I
write.

'Believe me,

'Your affectionate aunt,

'MARY CARROL ABBOTT.'

'What time am I to start for London,
Willie?' I asked, as I concluded.

'The best train leaves at noon. You will
not be afraid to go home, then, dear?'

'No,' I said, unhesitatingly; 'I remember
nothing of the master but kindness, and I
expect nothing else now. I agree with Aunt
Marshall; I ought to go to him. I will be
ready punctually to-morrow, Willie.'

CHAPTER IX.

'HELEN,' I said, 'what do you think of Willie ?'

'He seems—amiable, Harry.'

'Amiable!' I repeated, energetically. 'You discontented girl, can't you find anything better to say for him than that? Most people are amiable the first time you see them !'

'My dear Harry, you can't expect everybody to see such a paragon and wonder in your brother as you do. You, yourself, seem to me much better looking, much cleverer, much nicer everyhow;'—pointing her shaft by a sweeping lift and droop of her lashes.

I remonstrated : ' Child, how can you be so absurd ? Why, I haven't a solitary beauty but my dark eyes ; and Willie is thoroughly handsome.'

But it is not in human nature to reject entirely a sweet draught of flattery held to one's lips by a beloved hand. I felt gratified by the thought that Helen loved me enough to be blind where I was concerned. Such self-deluding mortals are we !

' Willie,' I queried, as we rode up to London the next day, the carriage being otherwise empty permitting the pleasant posture of my head on Willie's shoulder, and my hand upon his head, while both his arms were around me ; ' Willie, what do you think of Helen ?'

' Hem—I could not say after an evening's acquaintance.'

' But you must have some sort of a notion,' I expostulated.

'Yes? Well, I would rather have you for my sister than Miss Manseargh.'

'That's because I have this remarkable nose that Aunt Marshall talks about as a kind of natural patent of nobility. It's because I *am* your sister, silly boy. That isn't telling me what you think of Helen.'

'That is what I shall call making a diagnosis without inquiring into the symptoms. You should ask me, " Is it in the nose?" not jump to a conclusion, and of course you have made a mistake through being so unscientific. It is not the nose, but my dear old Harry altogether, face and mind, whom I place above Miss Manseargh.'

And I, undreaming of the mysteries of the human heart, marvelled inly at this peculiar coincidence of opinion between Helen and Willie.

I cannot understand how what I believe to be the fact is to be explained, that the mind can reproduce as vividly the small

annoyances and vexations, the minor miseries
and pains of existence, as it can those which
seemed overwhelming at the time of their
occurrence. Storms of feeling have rent my
soul; fate has placed me´in circumstances as
cruel, and has left me in as utter wretchedness, as I imagine a human being possibly
could have endurance for—let the reader decide whether this has but been so when I
have finished my history; and yet my memory
recalls certain days of small things, wherein I
endured petty annoyance or discomfort, more
distinctly than it will revivify those intense
storms, those great agonies of my life. To
such an extent is this carried in at least my
own mind that I verily believe that if I were
asked to remember the most wretched hours
I have ever passed, my instinct, my emotional
faculties, would exclaim in my mind for some
of these small miseries; and it would be a few
seconds—an appreciable interval of time—

before my reason would remind me that the great passions of grief which I have known *must* have caused me hours of deeper wretchedness than these puny aggravations did. How is it? I can only suggest that the atoms of the brain which are stirred by these great feelings and miseries are so violently agitated that they are, so to speak, stunned; or that they are driven with such force that they are to a certain extent fixed and immovable, and resist for an instant the effort of the will to reproduce gently their old exertions.

But this is not precisely light reading. And as the only aim of my work should be— as ask the novel readers, should it not?— to tell my story, I with penitence take up my thread, which, nevertheless, I have scarcely dropped; for the whole of the passage which has just preceded this was suggested by and connected with the reflection, How miserable that journey to Exeter was! Willie took me straight to the house of our uncle Henry, where I was made comfortable for the night. The next morning the old gentleman who was to be my escort, and who had kindly hastened his leaving London by a day or two that he might fulfil that office to oblige my uncle Marshall, made his appearance at the unpleasantly early hour of eight o'clock. The train by which he intended we should travel left Paddington at nine, and he had arrived early that he might be secure of my getting ready; for he was a precise old gentleman, and must not miss a train any more than he must miss shaving. This one little fact made me suspect that he was not an agreeable old gentleman; and my suspicion by-and-by changed to certainty. He made me hurry and bustle over the first meal of the day; a course of proceeding which is, in itself, enough to turn pleasure into discontent for the next twelve hours.

Willie appeared to go to the station, looking jaded and weary. He had been watching all night a case of 'acute laryngitis,' which, following upon his railway journeys, had tired him out. Nevertheless, the dear fellow, knowing how much I should like to see him, had come to take me to the train. I mention this chiefly because he wanted to buy me a book to read, and the old gentleman so angrily said, Why, he had got everyone of the papers, that we did not have the book.

You can see I feel a little spiteful about that old gentleman. So I do; his grave, clerical appearance is unpleasant to my vision in memory. He helped to make me uncomfortable.

I opine that he looked upon women as so many men do—as beings to be protected and kept under. He very carefully made of his portmanteau a hassock for my feet; he consulted my wishes about the window; and he

placed upon the opposite seat biscuits, and
sherry in a flask, and invited me to help myself therefrom when I might feel disposed.
But he seated himself at the far end of the
carriage, and when I spoke to him, he snubbed
me. It was not that he did not like to talk;
for he gossiped unremittingly to a gentleman
who travelled in our carriage between two
stopping-points; only he would not talk to me.

He had all the papers. Yes; and he sat
upon them. He began by giving me the
Times supplement, while he himself perused
the rest of that journal. There was nothing
in the advertisement sheet to interest me;
and so I sat, looking blankly at it, and thinking. Presently, he handed me the body of
the paper. But I discovered that he had
carefully cut out various paragraphs, which, I
suppose, he concluded I should not see. So I,
in dignified disgust, laid it down, and awaited
no more of his driblets of Bowdlerized news.

So I thought and thought of poor James, lying in his foreign grave, placed there by careless hands, and dying among strangers, hundreds of miles from our Devonshire home. When my vivid imagination had made this sufficiently terrible and distinct to thoroughly impress my mind, I began to think of where and what I was going to. The longer I thought, the more the prospect of facing my father alarmed and depressed me. I had not dreaded it at all before; but now, the coming meeting became quite a gigantic apprehension. Then the sun went in, and dulness came over the face of things, and the rain cheerlessly drizzled. And the wind rose, and moaned as a summer wind had no right to do. And the country seemed to be bleak and bare. And, as I said in the beginning, I was wretched altogether.

Never was traveller more delighted to reach his goal than was I to alight at

Exeter. My escort took me to an hotel, where he ordered the post carriage which was to convey me to Abbey Castle ; and while it was preparing he invited me to take some dinner. But, inasmuch as he remarked that there was soup and roast mutton ready, —which was fortunate, because there could not be anything better for a young lady fresh from school than roast mutton,—I decided that I should prefer getting out of the company of this reverend bore as quickly as possible, and declined dinner.

Sorrow, apprehension, hunger, and fatigue were therefore my travelling companions in the hotel brougham. Miserable crew ! Any one of them alone will banish happiness ; but they work best together, the presence of each giving tenfold strength to the others.

Nor, I conjecture, could worse external circumstances be devised for their unfortunate victim than those in which I was

placed. The country, during rain, presents
a much more dismal appearance than the
streets of a town. The rain dripping from
trees which seem to droop and shudder
under its violence, the broad expanse of
sodden field, the filthy roads, the ditches
of stagnant water incited to send forth
horrible odours, are peculiar to that part of
creation with which man has not interfered.
Even the mere blank solitude of fields is
an element of suffering unknown to those
who get through their rainy days in town.
Desolation is the attribute of wet rurality.

Petty misery—upon which cavilling critics
may perhaps accuse me of having written a
chapter, seeing that it has been perforce my
chief record for to-day—is much more un-
hinging to the nerves than a great gush of
trouble. Therefore, by the time my two
hours' drive was completed, as far as to the
gate of the grounds of Abbey Castle, I had

lost the necessary courage to have my unex-
pected brougham driven up to the front
entrance, and preferred dismissing the vehicle
and walking up on foot, in the rain, to the
back door.

The first announcement of my identity had
to be made at the lodge, where I left my
luggage. But the neat little girl in a servant's
cap knew nothing whatever about me, and
accepted the charge of my boxes in a state
of mystification.

When I had passed up the familiar avenue,
and through the shrubbery to the kitchen
entrance, the same thing was the case.
There were three servants there, but all were
strangers to me, and stared at my bedraggled
attire in wonderment.

I asked for Mrs. Stillingfleet, and one of
them went and found her.

I had grown completely out of the good
housekeeper's knowledge. But when I had

told her that I was the master's daughter, Henrietta, she discovered that I really had not altered much, and that I 'favoured the family—especially in the nose ;' and she was right down glad I was come, for the master was very much cut up. He was in the morning-room, she added ; and thither I directed my footsteps.

The rain made the day chilly, and my father had a small, blazing fire alight. Although it was only half-past five on a summer evening, it was so dark a day that, as he sat with his back towards the window, I saw him far more by the flickering light of the fire than by that of the dull skies.

How well I remembered that stately figure, and that stern face, with its hereditary fine Roman nose, which my own features reproduced. And how well I could understand the meaning of the listless attitude, the slight stoop of the shoulders. I stood and watched him through the half-

·open door for fully five minutes. Then he turned his head, and saw me in the hall. Sympathy, and the instinct of relationship, accomplished for me what my thoughts had for so long failed to arrange. Before he could speak I was beside his chair, kneeling down so that my face was on a level with his, and resting my hand upon his arm.

'Father—I am Harry!'

'Harry, my child?' he asked, fixing a piercing glance upon me.

'Yes, father, I have come because poor James is dead; they tell me my mother said I was to be a comforter to you one day; won't you let me be, father?' and with characteristic impulsiveness, I dared to embrace his grand old head between my hands.

He looked at me firmly for a moment; then his composure broke down; his eyes filled with tears, and his lips quivered; but for my sole and sufficient answer, he wrapped his arms around me, and drew me to his breast.

CHAPTER X.

BEFORE I retired for the night to the room which Mrs. Stillingfleet had prepared for me, I had fully succeeded in substituting my existing individuality for that of the singular little character called Harry, and aged eleven, who had lived in my father's affections all through those years. I hope I do not misjudge the master while I believe that his grief was intensified by the fact that his long-laid plans had come to naught, that his determinations were made futile. My birth had annoyed him, because he had laid plans and had made determinations which were destined to come to grief over my sex. The death of his son frustrated other plans, and the natural grief of the father was intensified by the humiliation of the resolute mind, finding its own strength of will of no account. Yet I see nothing inexplicable in the fact that my coming to him at this juncture was a comfort to him, and that he was more disposed at this moment to become permanently reconciled to my sex than he could have been under other circumstances. Perhaps it seems paradoxical to say that the occurrence of a second misfortune made the most favourable opportunity for reconciling him to the first one; but I do not think it is so really. There must be a certain amount of humility in a mind which will consciously 'make the best of things.' To find that its most skilful plans and its strongest determinations are nothing availing against Fate is the bitterest knowledge to a proud spirit; and its instinctive rebellion prevents it from admitting the possibility that, after all, there may be other good than that which it designed. But, at the same time, a consolation extracted from the grief itself is both the most natural and most efficacious of consolations. When, therefore, my warm sympathetic nature offered itself to soothe the wound in my father's heart, it was the most fitting balm ; for he was, in receiving it, obtaining consolation from the failure of his plans, while, at the same time, his pride could avoid the consciousness that this was really what was happening. And not only was I especially fitted to be his consoler, and hence to be taken into his full favour, by this fact, but also by the natural warmth and strength of my sympathetic feelings, and by the bond between us of blood, and even by our relationship of father and daughter ; for I cannot doubt that the Lawgiver of the Israelites was in the right when he held that sex has influence between the very nearest

relatives. For all this, O beloved general
reader, I entreat you to blame the critics;
who would have declared that I had stated
a psychological improbability, had I been content to leave standing unexplained the true
statement, which will be sufficient for you,
that my father received me gladly, and was
comforted by me, and soon loved me truly,
and was proud of his unwished-for, unintended
daughter, in her womanhood.

And now I proceed with my story, in the
hope and belief that it will be long before I
shall need thus to travel into problems of
causation again.

'And have you forgotten all your medical
learning, Harry?' asked my father, as we sat
together after breakfast, on the day following
my arrival. I had, at his bidding, given him
an account of my studies, and a general idea
of my life for the past seven years.

'Oh, no, sir!' I replied, falling back so naturally into the old style of address to the master. 'You know you sent me "Ellis" and "Armstrong," and I read them several times at intervals, and "Taylor on Poisons," which was the only medical book I had for a long time, I know almost by heart at this moment. If any one here should get poisoned, sir, I have the symptoms of the various drugs, and the proper antidotes, quite at my finger-ends.'

'Ah! what a student you could be!' sighed my father. 'What a pity you will not be able to begin just as Willie finishes, so that he might give you a helping hand during his last term, as your uncles William and Henry did in their time.'

'Yes: dear old Willie,' said I, smiling; 'there is nothing I should like better than to begin under his eye, when he is in his last year, and I am sure he would be pleased.'

'What a fine man you would have made!'

continued my father, in sober mournfulness. 'Your face is strong in its expression, and you have the Abbott nose larger and finer than any of your brothers except Lynton.'

'Has Lynton *the* nose well developed?' exclaimed I. 'You know, sir, I have not seen him at all for eight years. I have no idea what he is like. However, it is fortunate that he has that particular feature in good prominence, since it is he who will have to transmit it to the next generation of the principal branch of the family.'

'He has been on the Continent a year now,' said my father; 'but even when he was here last he looked nearly as old as I do, though he is not quite thirty. His hair is shaded with grey. And, as you say, it is he who has to keep up the family name. I wish he would marry, and settle down here, Harry.'

'He is older than you were when you married, is he not?'

'Oh, yes! I married at twenty-five, my dear, and am only seven-and-twenty years older than Lynton. Now, none of your brothers have shown any disposition to marry young—except Marshall—Ah!'

My father ended with a long-drawn sigh, and a very grave and displeased look. I knew scarcely anything of my only sister-in-law. Two years before, my Aunt Marshall had told me that my brother was married, without the consent or knowledge of his father, and that his wife was much beneath us. After giving me which information, she had peremptorily closed the subject.

At this present moment Marshall was Vicar of Apsland, the old incumbent having only had the gift of the living from my father to 'keep it warm' until my brother should be ready to take the occupancy. Marshall and his wife were, therefore, established at the Vicarage, and, as I should have to meet this new sister-in-law very soon, it occurred to me that I ought to know something about her. I ventured to interrupt my father's grave reverie with a hint.

'My aunt has told me very little of Marshall's marriage, father.'

' It was a very great trial to me,' said my father, coming out of his abstraction. ' What did Mrs. Marshall tell you ?'

' Nothing but that she was not a fit match for one of us. . . . I suppose I must go down and see them soon ?'

' Yes, my dear.'

' And ought I not to know a little more about it first, sir ?' I asked, rather timidly, since he continued silent.

' Yes, you should; but I wish Mrs. Marshall had spared me the telling of the story,' responded my father, with knit brows. ' But, since I must :—Well, Harry, your brother took a good position in the pass-list of his

college, three years ago, and might have had a
fellowship forthwith, in which to remain until
he could take priest's orders. He wanted to
decline it, but the Dean and I insisted, and
so he had to confess at last that he had been
married for the previous six months ; and,
worse than that, his first child was three
months old or so. She—his wife—was the
daughter of a man who had been an insig-
nificant curate, and she is tolerably well
educated. But she absolutely knows nothing
of her grandfather ; and her mother was an
extremely low, ignorant person. Her father
was dead. He must have married below even
his station. Then they were very poor ; did
plain needlework for a living ; the mother
even went out charing, sometimes, I believe.
Of course he did wisely to marry the girl at
last. We can more easily condone this marriage than we could have hushed up——
Well, Harry, it's a thing I can't talk to

you about. You're not my son really, you
know; but . . . . . I don't understand how a
fellow like Marshall came ever to be carried
off his feet.'

Neither did I.

' Is she pretty, sir ?' I asked.

' Well—after a fashion perhaps. . . . . No,
it would be gross flattery to call her pretty.
She has an innocent, juvenile face, that might
be rather taking ; though I shouldn't have
guessed that sort of thing would entrap a
fellow like Marshall.'

Again I agreed with my father. Marshall's
marriage now presented itself to me as equally
deplorable and mystifying. A Mrs. Abbott
who did not know anything of her grandfather, and whose mother did charing !—
Dreadful ! And underbred, and not pretty !
It was equally wonderful !

I may as well say at once that, though I
afterwards learned the true story of my

brother's *mésalliance* from the lips of his unfortunate wife, I cannot relate it here. It would be scouted as too black a tale to be true. For good reasons, I decline to enlighten the world farther upon the point.

The words, 'You are not my son, really, Harry,' seemed to have taken my father's thoughts back to the point from whence he had started ; for when he spoke next, after a moment's pause, he was there.

' You would look a great deal better in a coat and hat than in that sort of thing,' was what he said; 'that sort of thing' contemptuously indicating my light morning dress and long curls.

' I wonder if I should,' I laughed, looking at his serious face.

' You had better try,' responded my father, instantly. 'Come, I'll bring in my coat and hat, and you shall try them on eh ?'

The suggestion presented itself to me as an excellent piece of fun ;—the very opposite from what it appeared to the master.

' Certainly, sir ;' said school-girl merriment.

My father brought into the morning-room a black frock-coat and a high hat, and I, with much amusement, proceeded to induct myself into the former.

' You ought to have a white front,' remarked my father, who stood on the opposite side of the hearth surveying me.

' No, sir; this will do,' I said, unfastening the white muslin bow at my throat; ' if you will lend me your scarf pin.' I tucked the ends of my tie down straight, after the fashion of the ' bands ' of John Wesley and his clerical contemporaries; then, fastening the two edges together with my father's pin, not a bad substitute for a ' dickey ' was formed. I buttoned the coat up tightly so far as it closed; and turned all my curls up on to the top of my head, fixing them there by putting on the hat. I laughed a little at my own reflection in the glass, and then turned to the master to be inspected.

'Capital!' was his verdict; 'you look a fine manly young fellow, Harry; your features are much too large for a beautiful woman; but they would be——'

His sentence was abruptly cut short by a rap at the door.

'Come in,' said my father, a little startled into thoughtlessness; and the door immediately opened to admit—not a woman servant, but a gentlemanly-looking young man, a complete stranger to me. I blushed violently, and sat down immediately on the couch behind me, hoping to escape his notice. My father faced the door, and placed himself in front of me; but the intruder saw me instantly—his eyes swept over the strange

medley of my attire, though, with innate good
taste, he immediately removed his glance,
and looked at me no more while he stayed in
the room. I did not venture even to remove
my hat, but sat, feeling very foolish, until he
had said what he had to say, and went out
with my father. Then I removed the
manly garb with all speed, and had
just finished tying up my bow when my
father re-entered the room, drawing on his
gloves.

'Well, Harry, we were surprised,' he said,
taking up his hat.

'Yes, sir ; whoever is that young gentleman ?'

'That ?—only my steward ; I have had
him for two years. The management of the
home farm, and of the estate altogether,
grew quite too much for me ; and as Lynton did not seem disposed to stay here and
help with it, I decided to employ a pro-

fessional agent—some one better than the old bailiff—to look after things in general under me. I want you to be civil to him ; he's a very respectable young man—I wish you had been in fitting attire for me to present him to you just now. There he is ; you have no objection to my calling him in to introduce him, I suppose, my dear ?'

'None whatever, father.'

So my father opened the window, and called ' Brown,' and the young man turned from the gardener, to whom he was speaking, and came round through the hall into the room.

'My dear Harry, permit me to make known to you Mr. Brown, my steward. Brown, this is Miss Abbott, my only daughter.'

Mr. Brown looked at me now ; a full clear look, out from a pair of bright grey eyes.

He bowed as low as I desired, and said he was very glad to have the honour. Then he and my father went about their business.

CHAPTER XI.

WHEN my father came in to luncheon, I asked him whether he did not think I ought, in common courtesy, to walk down during the afternoon to see Marshall and his wife. He assented, and immediately after the meal sat down and wrote a note telling my brother that I had arrived at Abbey Castle, and that I should call at the Vicarage in about an hour. This note he sent at once, by a man; and I sat down with him for a little while that the Vicarage people might have due time to prepare for my advent.

In this interval we talked, among other things, about Mr. Brown. He was the son

of a labourer, living not far off, my father
said, and had been given the rudiments of
education by the charity of his clergyman,
who had seen something bright in the
boy. Brown had followed ordinary agricul-
tural labourers' employment for a few years
after; but the same good friend, the clergyman, had taken him as his under-gardener,
and had afterwards given him entire charge
of his small farm. Brown had risen by
degrees thence, till, at seven-and-twenty, he
became my father's steward. He was an
excellent agriculturist, said the master, a
good man of business, and, what was far
more extraordinary, quite a gentleman in
manners, habits, and tastes, and had so
improved his own education as to become a
good classical and general scholar. He owed
it all, my father added, to the kindness of
the reverend gentleman, who had not only
had him educated, but had, some years after,

made quite an associate of him, both in general parish work and, to a degree, personally.'

' And now he is constantly with my father,'
said I, complimentarily, ' it would be strange
if his manners and tastes did not receive the
highest degree of polish that they can bear.'

The sagacious reader will readily conclude
that all this would not have been transferred
to my pages without Mr. Brown were to
prove hereafter a somewhat considerable
person therein.

Imperative business took my father in a
different direction, and I set out alone for
the Vicarage. I knew the somewhat long
route most perfectly, and travelling it carried
my thoughts back to the happy days of my
boy-girlhood, and to the warm affection
which had joined Willie and me in every
pursuit, from our medical studies down to
the setting of our hens. Absorbed in memo-
ries, I went on until I reached a gate, the

13—2

unfastening of which compelled my thoughts
to return to things present. I had made a
short detour off my father's estate, and was
now coming upon it again. This was one of
its boundary gates. It was too tall for the
most daring sportsman, and was padlocked,
but foot-passengers obtained admission to the
field through a small wooden-barred wicket
which opened in the large gate. I lifted up
the latch of this wicket, and was about to
perform the feat of clambering up to the
aperture and through the same, when lo ! an
enemy appeared. Or should not I rather,
in the name of sacred justice, say—he who
was before me in the field rose up, and
bellowed his intention to retain the absolute
possession ? His eyes gleamed red, and uprose
his tail, while in the air his pointed horns he
tossed, and lifted from off the earth his
powerful hoofs. So the gigantic bull hurled
at me his defiance !

So I was kept off my father's lands and away from my brother's house by a presumptuous bull! The situation was annoying, but I saw its comic side. The bull was evidently, however, a determined animal, and told me so by his various tossings and flingings, as I stood and contemplated him through the reclosed wicket. I would have reasoned the question with him, but I had neither the thick stick nor the strong arm which are requisite preliminaries to discussing a point of right of way with a bull.

Just as *statu quo* was beginning to get too much for my patience, and I was wondering if to be gored to death were really very unpleasant—going back not having occurred to me yet—I heard a step in the lane behind me, from which I was a few steps removed. I turned, and beheld Mr. Brown proceeding along. He saw me at that moment, and, recognising me, raised his hat; then, seeing that I was in some difficulty, came toward me.

'You seem destined to find me in what a French novelist would call "situations,"' said I, making the best of the position.

'I hope I can assist you, Miss Abbott.' This just as he reached the gate. Then, perceiving the bull, he elevated his eyebrows, and stopped.

'When I was at home,' I continued, 'this field was the common pathway between Wilton village and the church and Vicarage. Is that altered? for, if not, I should think it is scarcely safe to keep an animal subject to such fits of fury in the field.'

'He has no right whatever in the field, miss,' said Brown; 'it is still the pathway to the Vicarage, and this brute has broken out of the next field, through over there, where perhaps you can see the bars are thrown down. I must drive him back there.'

He looked about; but the hedges presented none but small sticks. However, Brown selected the largest and prickliest, and armed only therewith, approached the wicket before which I stood. The animal inside, I conclude, overheard the decision; he became more lively even than before. Pointing his chin higher in the air, standing alternately on his hind and fore-legs and flourishing the spare pair more vigorously, he proclaimed his opinion thereupon.

'Might I ask you, Miss Abbott,' said the steward, 'to walk just a few steps round into the lane, while I clear the path for you in this field."

I glanced significantly from the bull and his weapons to the man and his branch of a stick. 'You mean,' I replied, with the bluntness of impetuosity, 'will I get out of the way, that the bull may kill you without my seeing the murder ?'

'Not at all,' he said, smiling—a full frank smile, I noticed—' if the bull will not yield to me, I shall retire, and bring assistance to deal with him.'

' But if it rushes at you,' I retorted, ' how do you think you can get out ?'

' Through the wicket.'

' But you cannot,' I asserted, ' you cannot safely get over this high step, and through this narrow opening, either one way or the other.'

' But what is to be done ?' he asked, pausing to appeal to common sense. ' Even if I were willing that you should go back, or right round by Wilton, without my even attempting to remove the obstacle out of your path, it would not be doing my duty to go away even to fetch assistance, leaving the brute out here, where he may attack some defenceless old woman, perhaps.'

' You must open the big gate.'

'Pardon me—indeed I must not, miss; the bull might rush through there before I could prevent him, if I once went away from the gate, and injure you.'

We stood for a moment and surveyed each other's resolute faces.

'See, Mr. Crown,' I said, presently, 'one of us must give way, and I assure you it shall not be me. I will not move from in front of this wicket until you promise me you will not attempt to get through it, while you are alone.'

'Really—I am very sorry—I should be most pleased if I could do anything you desire me, Miss Abbott; but in this particular instance I *must not* obey. I cannot open the whole gate, and expose you to so much danger, and I should never forgive myself if I went away without even trying to drive this brute back, and then some poor old creature lost her life through my cowardice.'

I immediately noted, and was pleased by the greater strength of his expressions about the possibility of harm befalling one of the poor old pensioners of the Vicarage than of myself, his master's freshly-appeared daughter. It was generous that he should remember the age and decrepitude of a poverty-stricken Darby or Joan, rather than the rank and position of my young active self. Brown had evidently not improved his standing by mean servility to his superiors.

'I won't be hurt,' I told him. 'You unlock the whole of the gate, and go in at it, and I will hold it in my hand, keeping it closed against the bull, but ready to pull it open and shut it to again, if he should attack you, and you need to hurry out.'

He hesitated and looked very doubtful; but I urged so strongly, and repeated my determination so decidedly, that at length, having stipulated that I would not open the gate if

there were any chance of the bull getting
through, Brown produced the key from his
pocket, unfastened the padlock, and passed
through the gate into the field. I stood holding the gate so that I could readily open it
a little way; and watching the course of events
with my heart beating high, and my lips tightly
closed in excitement. Thus began the tug of
war. The man walks into the field about
half-a-dozen foot-lengths; the bull perceives
him, and, dancing high into the air, meditates
a rush at him; but, seeing the man stand
firmly, is astonished, and pauses to wonder.
They stand, for the amazement of the bull to
subside, for a full minute. Fatal minute! in
it the firm resolute bearing of the man, and
that wonderful magnetic power by which man
has dominion over the brute, assert their influence on the marveller. His tail is lowered,
his attitude more uncertain, when he recovers
himself. His spring is more subdued, when

he gathers himself together, and performs a *grand rond* about his adversary. The man turns upon his heel, and keeps him off by the continual exertion of the power which was established during that hesitating moment. *Grand rond* is repeated five times; then astonishment once more enters the bullish brain, and he stops to survey the undaunted bearing of his opponent. The man selects this moment for the bold attack; with his small stick upreared he advances upon his foe; the bull, surprised, retreats, retreats twenty foot-lengths, and then—humanity victorious—the brute fairly turns tail, and rushes full speed before his pursuing conqueror, into his own field. Brown calmly replaces the broken hedge sticks, spends several minutes in fastening them up, then turns to where I have come up to watch and applaud.

The emotions with which I had stood 'spectatress of the fight' are not reproducible.

I was wrapped up in the struggle of reason
and human will with brute force. When the
bull was safely back in his own domain, I
aroused, to find myself standing with every
muscle drawn tense, and my teeth so tightly
set that they were aching in expostulation.
I walked quickly across the field, and was
standing beside the victor when he turned
away from wedging in the pushed-out boards.

'Why did you come into the field until I
came back to tell you he was safely caged,
miss?' he said; the title of respect on his lips
sounding, by the way, no more nor no less
obeissant than a Frenchman's ' *ma'amselle.*'

' I was not so frightened as that!' I
laughed.

'You have all the courage of your race,
Miss Abbott,' he said, looking at me with
respectful admiration. 'I do not suppose one
young lady in a thousand could be found to
act as you did.'

'I did nothing at all wonderful,' I returned;
'but *you*—that animal might have killed you,
although I held the gate ready, as he certainly
would have done if you had been called upon
to clamber through the wicket. You are very
brave, indeed;' and my eyes told him, as my
lips could not, how I appreciated that bravery.

'You praise me too much,' he replied; 'I
didn't expect he would attempt to hurt me;
a sane man ought to be always able to conquer a brute who is only out of temper, miss.
When they are quite mad, of course there is
nothing to be done with them; but in such a
case as this, any man who knows animals
could do what I have done.'

Which assertion I negatived by a little
deprecatory shake of my head. Then, as he
stood with his hat in his hand, awaiting what
I might desire, I asked: 'Do you think there
are any more bulls between here and the
Vicarage, Mr. Brown?'

'Indeed I hope there are not, miss,' he replied, smiling, 'or the master will take away my character for carefulness. But this same bull's field runs parallel with the next. If you will permit me, I will just step over to the stile, and see that he has not broken through there.'

'We can walk over together,' I said, partly impelled by my father's 'Be civil to him,' partly by my own unexamined impulses.

So we went across the field, side by side, and talking. The steward assisted me over the stile with very un-labourlike care and elegance, and walked along the footpath beside me, with his eye upon the hedge; but when we came to the next stile, I was recounting to him the feats of the marvellous Milo; and as he seemed to be going on, I forgot to inquire whether this was his road. So we went together through the next two fields, until we came in sight of the Vicarage,

and I had only one field more and the church-
yard to traverse. Then my escort stopped,
and raising his hat again, said:

'With your permission I will leave you now;
there is no more danger to be feared between
here and the Vicarage.'

'Have you come right out of your way
with me?' I exclaimed; 'I am so sorry.'

'It is such a pleasure as I do not often
enjoy,' he began; then flushed a little bit
under the consciousness of speaking too freely.
'I am very obliged to you, miss,' he added,
'for permitting me to see that you were not
molested any more. I will take care that the
hedge is attended to immediately, so that
it will be quite safe before you pass back
again.'

I bowed, and wished him 'Good morning,'
and we went our respective ways. Then
I reflected that this good-looking young man,
to whom I had been talking familiarly, was,

only a few years ago, a common farm labourer! But there was nothing in his manners and appearance to remind one unpleasantly of the fact. He knew his proper position, and with true pride he retained it; equally without offensive servility and offensive familiarity. Moreover, I had that passionate admiration for physical bravery which is common among women, and which would frequently lead them to perform deeds of the greatest courage and daring if they were not taught that timidity is as much a virtue in their sex as it is a vice in the other.

Altogether, my impressions of Brown were very favourable, and he was *an individual* to me thenceforward.

CHAPTER XII.

'Is Mr. Abbott in?' I asked the servant who replied to my knock at the front door of Apsland Vicarage.

'No, miss; he has not been in since morning, first thing.'

'Mrs. Abbott is, I suppose?'

'Yes, miss.'

'Then, will you please tell her I wish to see her?' I asked, attempting to enter the hall.

'Mrs. Abbott does not receive visitors, miss,' said the woman, standing still in my path.

'But she will see me,' said I; and I passed

her into the hall, feeling a little annoyed at this reception. 'She expects me. Be good enough to tell her, please.'

'Who shall I say, miss ?' asked the servant, overawed, probably, by the combination of this assertion with my Abbott nose. (I do not jest, please. That nose has often been of service to my dignity.)

'Miss Abbott,' I answered ; and the woman went to a door opening out of the hall, tapped at it, and entered through it.

The fact was, I could not help feeling a great deal more haughtily towards this sister-in-law than I did towards my father's steward. It seemed to me infinitely more distressing to recognise a sister in this lowly-born clergyman's daughter than to acknowledge the acquired rank of the farm labourer. This, of course, because the one claimed equality with my family, while the other still remained far our inferior. I waited calmly in the hall

while the servant announced me as Miss
Abbott; whereas, if I had felt differently disposed, my natural warm-heartedness would at
least have made me introduce myself as her
' sister.'

The door through which the servant dis-
appeared re-opened presently, and the woman
asked me to walk in. I did so, and found that
the room had three occupants : a little girl
about four years old, a baby (sleeping on the
couch), and a lady, who stood in an uncertain
attitude beside the fire-place.

' What a tiny little thing!' said my thoughts
to myself, immediately ; ' why, she isn't more
than half my size.'

And, in truth, she was *not* much more ;
small, and now thin, though she had evidently
once been plump. Hers was one of those
childish, innocent-looking faces which are
enchanting in youth and happy healthiness,
but absolutely ugly under other conditions.

This face was haggard and pale, with large black swollen circles under the eyes. The untended aspect of her hair, and the soiled and tumbled condition of her brown-holland dress, struck unpleasantly upon me at once.

This figure stood with her hands tightly clasped together, and a half-frightened look in her eyes ; and seemed to have not a word to say. I also was somewhat embarrassed ; for complete readiness of tact comes only with practice in society. But she forced me to speak first.

' You have received my father's letter, I suppose ?'

' No,' she replied, with an ugly nervous twist of her lips, and in unassured tones. ' There was a letter brought down for Marshall from the Castle, but I did not open it.'

' Then, I have to introduce myself to you,' I said. ' I am Mr. Abbott's daughter—your

husband's sister Henrietta. You have probably heard him speak of me ?'

' I—no—that is—I mean I have heard him
—your name,' she stammered. · I suppose
you want to see him.'

She was so evidently frightened, there was
such a look of appeal hiding, as it were, in her
eyes, that she reminded me irresistibly of a
bird fluttering in a captor's hand. So I
pitied her, instead of resenting her ill-bred
speech.

' What time will he be in ?' I asked ; *not*
having myself enough of that polite equanimity which can return conversational good
for evil, to assure her that I had chiefly
desired to make her sisterly acquaintance.

' ' I do not know. He never tells me where
he is going,' with a small shake of her
shoulders, fascinating once, no doubt ; now
almost comic. ' He may be in at any
moment.'

'Will he not be in to dinner ?' I asked.

'We dined at one; and he told me not to expect him home then. He has been out since about ten.'

'Well, I have till about five o'clock to spare,' I said; 'and I will wait until then to see if he comes—if you will permit me,' I added.

'O, I shall be pleased, I'm sure,' said my hostess. 'Will you come into the drawing-room to sit down ?'

I protested that this room would do very nicely; but she insisted, and so we went across the hall into an opposite apartment, the baby going with us. It served as a fortunate resource. Women seem always able to find something to say to babies, and this one supplied me now, in my hour of need, with something to say to prevent awkward silence. Just as the topic began to get exhausted, the front door opened, and a man's foot stepped into the hall.

'There is Marshall,' said his wife, in a subdued and hurried tone, and with her face assuming a new expression of half alarm, half expectation. She rose from her seat, and stood, as though uncertain what to do, until the step had proceeded half-way up the stairs. Then she went quickly to the door, and out, closing it behind her. But I could hear, through the door, the little conversation.

'Marshall!'

'Well?'—a gruff, hard snap.

'Come down here, will you?'

'Why?'

'You are wanted.'

'By you?'

'No; your sister is here.'

'My sister! What did you let me get so far up for, before you told me?'

Then he descended the stairs : there was the sound of a few rapid words from him just outside the door, spoken in a tone too low to reach my ear, and he came in to me.

Came, different in many respects from the Marshall Abbott of seventeen years of age. Clad in the long coat of a priest, and closely shaven, but so black-haired that he could not be said to present a clean face, the *tout ensemble* of this young cleric of twenty-five was very different from that of the boy-student. This was apparent at a glance ; but, when one came to study him, more real differences of *extérieure* were discoverable. The extreme boniness of his face was no longer perceptible. The big bones were necessarily there, but they were concealed by—

'Padding round with flesh and fat,'

and their only effect was to make his face a little broad. His eyes, too, were deeply set,

but not buried in his head, as they had
appeared to be of old, except, as I by-and-by
discovered, in particular mental states. The
most noticeable feature now was the mouth.
His clean shaving left it perfectly free for
observation. The clear cutting of the upper
lip, with the deep division at its centre, was
common to most of my father's children;
but Marshall's mouth was all his own, by
reason of the upper lip's shortness, the
abrupt termination of its lips at their corners
without any softening out into curves, and,
above all, the depth of the lines drawn around
the mouth, both above and a little down to
the chin, and the general expression of
hardness, bitterness, and self-consciousness
mingled which it displayed.

As he came into the room, and held out
his hand to me, I thought instinctively of the
last time I had seen this brother. I remembered that autumn day at Dalestonbury, and

my murdered dog, killed, cruelly and remorselessly, by that very hand; and—I could not help it, strive as I would—a thrill of horror, a feeling of sickening repulsion, had to be overcome before I could lay my hand in his. More than that, looking into his face at the moment, I saw distinctly that he also remembered the circumstances under which we had last met.

'I am happy to see you, Henrietta,' he said, immediately; 'when did you come home?'

'Only yesterday evening,' I replied.

'It was very good of you to come down so early,' he went on, and there was the old surly tone, still existent, though marvellously trained and softened by intoning, by education, and, at this moment, by hollow politeness.

'And you have made Fanny's acquaintance?' he remarked, turning to where his little wife stood in the background. 'Fanny,' suddenly addressing her in slow, measured tones, such as one uses to a refractory horse, 'did you not know that my sister was coming?'

She gave a perceptible start when he spoke, and answered meekly, only, 'No, Marshall.'

'Father wrote a note to you, but you were out when it arrived,' I explained.

'I was going to suggest,' he continued, in the same manner, 'that it might have been well if you had looked a little more as you should look to meet my sister for the first time.'

'You cannot always be dressed "as you were going to a feast" when you have two babies to attend to, can you, Fanny?' said I, my benevolence aroused by her silent abasement, and my zeal endeavouring to propitiate him towards her by addressing her in friendly terms.

'She is not the nursemaid,' interposed her husband ; 'but she never looks decently tidy, much less as my wife should look.' By this time she seemed tolerably uncomfortable, and he condescended to leave her for a moment to extract the full suffering of this unkindness. 'I suppose you came down because of poor James's death, Henrietta ?'

'Yes,' I replied, briefly.

'How do you think our father is looking ?'

'Tolerably well.'

'And how did he receive you ?'

'Very kindly, indeed.' I was sympathising with what I conceived must be poor Fanny's humiliation, and not disposed to make long sentences to her tormentor. But I should have done her more service by keeping his attention away from her. It went back now.

'Did you know that I was a married man ?'

'Yes : Aunt Marshall just mentioned it.'

'Ah! she has never seen my wife; and you may guess I wish she never shall. How old should you think Fanny is?'

Again my good breeding revolted at the question, but I had not the social practice to evade it.

'About twenty-three,' I answered, therefore.

'You only say that because you know my age, and expect her to be a little younger,' he asserted, with perfect truth. 'I am sure that no one looking at her would imagine she was only that age. But it is only causeless weeping and wailing and complaining that have made her so old in appearance. How is Aunt Marshall, Henrietta?'

I briefly replied.

'She is a splendid woman, isn't she?' he said. 'She has such exquisite taste in all the arrangements of her house, as well as in her own dress. And I do detest a woman who has no taste in dress, or who is too ugly for dress to set off.'

'Yes, Aunt Marshall is unquestionably a fine woman,' I agreed.

'Fanny !' he exclaimed, suddenly facing round upon her. 'It appears you will not comply with an indirect request. I must speak out. Please to go and put on yourself a decent dress.'

'I must go,' I said, as the poor little girl turned to leave the room. 'Say "good-bye" to me, will you, Fanny.'

I went over to her, where she paused in the middle of the carpet. My heart had warmed to her now, and, as I took the hand she offered, I put my other arm round her, and kissed her forehead. She looked up at me with eyes from which big tears were slowly dropping over her wan cheeks. And I hope that, from that moment, she knew I was her friend.

'Why do you scold your wife in public ?' I asked the Rev. Marshall, in a low tone.

'My dear Henrietta,' he replied, so loudly that she must have heard every word, though she was outside the door before the sentence was concluded, 'I do not consider you the public. And even if I did, she deliberately angers me enough for both public and private remonstrances.'

He would walk with me as far as the entrance to our own park ; and all the way he kept the conversational ball rolling over indifferent casual matters with a skill which must have been of infinite service to him as a social clergyman. But when he left me at the park gates, and I walked on alone, re- flecting, I discovered that the dislike, the abhorrence, which not all these years had been able to remove from the memory of the boy Marshall in me, had been transferred in this hour to the present existing reality, the Rev. the Vicar of Apsland.

CHAPTER XIII.

THE Reverend Marshall Abbott, Vicar of
Apsleigh, was by no means unpopular in his
own neighbourhood.   His actions and his
words were generally exactly what those of a
gentleman in his position and of his profession ought to be.   He was never seen in
the hunting-field himself, but he took a keen
interest in the sport, and knew where the
hounds met and when, and had a host of
stories of remarkable runs and leaps, for the
country gentlemen who loved the subject.
He was a Justice of the Peace, and snubbed
offenders in the most approved style, when

their coats were ragged; and fined them a few shillings, while he almost apologised to them, when they happened to be clad in fine linen and broadcloth. He was the honorary chaplain of the workhouse, and visited the paupers sufficiently to maintain his character for clerical conscientiousness. Above all, his voice was soft and his manner composed of an agreeable mixture of deference and familiarity when he addressed a lady. Most of the neighbouring country gentry, therefore, preferred his church to the rival one of Delham, which had an old vicar who was guilty of following the hounds himself, who paid no attention to county business, and who was not—greatest crime of all—himself a scion of a county family, as was my brother.

I went to church with my father on the first Sunday after my arrival at home. Two mild elderly curates divided the service between them, and their vicar, who was young

enough to have been the son of either of
them, delivered the sermon. His text was
' In honour preferring one another,' and his
discourse was, as his female hearers mostly
said, ' sweet.'

About half-a-dozen carriages waited at the
church door, and the owners of most of them,
partly moved by curiosity as to whom I might
be, waited to shake hands with the Master of
Apsleigh. There were several young ladies,
and two or three young gentlemen, and the
grandees, their papas and mammas. While
I was still exchanging the first few words of
politeness with some of the former, and my
father was yet enduring with what equanimity
he might the condolences of the latter, the
vicar came out of the church door to where
we stood, to be greeted with effusion by all
parties except his father and sister.

' And how is poor dear Mrs. Abbott?' asked
one gushing young lady, throwing the ques-

tion over my shoulder, chiefly to draw the attention of the popular priest to herself.

A shade that might have been annoyance, or might have been sorrow, passed over Marshall's eyebrows, but he answered in his softest tones, and without any hesitation :

'How kind it is of you always to remember my poor wife ! I am sorry she is no better. It is a heavy cross, but we both try to submit with patience.'

He concluded with a most effective sigh.

'Ah !' responsively sighed the fair devotee ; then, whispering in my ear as I stood beside her : 'What heavenly patience the vicar shows under his heavy affliction, dear Miss Abbott. It improves us all to see it. Our little trials are so light before his. Have you seen your poor sister-in-law yet ?'

'Yes,' I replied simply, not a little mystified.

'It's all the spine, isn't it ?' chimed in a

second lady, who had overheard the last speech.

Marshall was listening, I suppose, with one ear, for he came to the rescue at once :

'My sister knows but little yet of my poor dear wife's condition,' he said, with a shade of severity in his tone, enough to quench his too talkative parishioners for the time ; 'and she will not, I am sure, give an unconsidered opinion which might make me miserable. We are such poor, impatient servants, we cannot always take the Lord's doings as mercy and goodness, and I cannot help hoping that Mrs. Abbott may yet recover at least sufficiently to receive our friends ; and even a careless hint to the contrary depresses me sadly.'

Again he finished with the effective sigh.

He had closed the topic.

'Does Marshall really give it out that his wife is too ill to be seen, sir?' I asked my

father, as we strolled home alone with each
other.

'Well,' said the master, unwillingly, 'I believe he does, Harry; and I can't interfere.
I hate to talk about them. It's the burden
of my life. But the fact is, she certainly did
behave in a most unbearable manner when
he did try to take her into company.'

'What did she do?' I asked; chivalrous
pity for the crushed little woman, and incur-
able detestation of my own brother, making me
inclined to doubt this statement if it rested
only on *his* authority.

'It is the sort of thing one can scarcely
explain definitely, although it is bad enough
to disgrace our position,' said my father, still
hesitatingly, and looking straight before him,
with his fine brows a little wrinkled. 'When
she first came, I wanted to make the best
of it, of course, and I had a few parties for
her at the Castle. My dear Harry—I don't

likc to say it, but she really could not—she could not even *eat* decently. She put her knife in her mouth, and she took a chicken-bone up in her fingers and scraped the meat off it. And she dropped her knife and fork and spoon and napkin regularly—Marshall declared she did it for her next neighbour to pick them up. And she always spilt her wine—and, in fact, I didn't think a girl who had been brought up above the gutter could behave so.'

'But, sir, was any of that bad enough to send her into complete retirement for? Wasn't it mostly nervousness, don't you think? And such things as scraping bones down—couldn't Marshall have taught her better at their own table, quietly?'

'Of course he tried that, my dear. Indeed, that was the worst of it. When she did one of these dreadful things she always looked down the table to her husband, just as a dog looks at his master after doing some wrong thing—the most terrified look, as though she expected to be immediately kicked. People noticed it and gossipped about it, I am sure, though one never hears what is said about one. The climax, Harry, was just a thing of that sort. One evening, I had Sir James and Lady Coffin—she is the greatest scandalmonger in Devon—and one or two other people to dinner, and I asked Fanny to come to play hostess; in fact, I had the party expressly to give her another trial, so to speak. I must tell you that Marshall had hinted to me that she was getting a habit of taking too much wine, both at dinner and other times. She sat facing me on this occasion, and beside Sir James Coffin. Before we had finished our soup she dropped her napkin, and, instead of ignoring it, or of quietly asking one of the servants for another, she pushed back her chair and picked it up for herself; then, in raising herself again, she knocked the handle of her knife or her fork against her glass of claret, and deluged the tablecloth with red wine.'

'She did not wait for her neighbour to pick it up *that* time, at all events,' I said, charitably seeking for a mitigating point in the indictment.

'Sir James is much too old and stout to stoop for a thing of comparatively small importance. But wait until I have finished my story, my dear. I assure you I never heard Marshall utter one word of reproof before, under any provocation. This time he was sitting quite near her, and he said only, in a very low tone, " Oh, Fanny !" And what do you think Mrs. Marshall Abbott did ? Looked at him with the most abject expression, and then burst into tears and loud sobs as she sat at the head of my table !'

'What did Marshall do ?'

'The worst part of the tale is to come. It was this that created the greatest *esclandre*. Marshall said, very quietly, "If you do not feel well, Fanny, you had better leave the table for a moment or two." She took no notice of this suggestion, and the other ladies were beginning to get up, as though to go to her assistance. Marshall left his seat, and went round to her and touched her on the shoulder. She looked up, and burst out, "Oh, Marshall, don't! It was an accident! I couldn't help it, indeed, Marshall!" This before half-a-dozen gossipping county women and my servants !'

'It was dreadful! Do you think it was talked about ?'

'Of course it was, Harry. You are an innocent fellow, fresh from school. You don't imagine what a delight something to gossip about is. Wait until you have seen a little more society, and then you will know how our name would be bandied about over every dinner-table, and whispered in every drawing-room for months.'

'What did Marshall say afterwards?'

'Well, he came and had a long talk with me about it. He told me plainly that he had several times found her in a state of intoxication when he came home after some hours' absence. I confess I was very much upset myself; and when he said that he was fully resolved not to receive any more visitors at the Vicarage, nor to permit her to pay visits, until he had tried, by care and kindness, to eradicate her worst habits, I offered no objection.'

'Care and kindness! Papa, do you think Marshall's kindness a reliable commodity?'

'Harry,' said my father, very seriously, 'you ought to know me better than to speak in such a manner. You ought to be sure that

I believe only kindness and gentleness will be shown by your brother to his wife; that I should not for a moment tolerate harshness and unkindness being shown by one of my sons to a woman; above all, when that woman is his wife. But you appear to misjudge your brother. I have never seen him show anything but really wonderful patience in this case.'

'Perhaps you are right, sir; Marshall and I had some not over pleasant passages when I saw him at Dalestonbury, years ago; and, possibly, the remembrance of that time does prejudice me against all that he does now.'

'Ha! what happened between you then?' asked my father, quickly.

But I, not seeing fit to take up so old a memory, evaded the question, and we walked in silence for a few moments; then my father added:

'Marshall is a man who has wonderful self-

control.   I have never seen anything cause a
violent outburst of passion in him.   He feels
very strongly, I don't doubt, but he can
restrain it perfectly.   There is no fear of his
natural grief and anger carrying him beyond
bounds.'

Ah! my dear father! Is it very self-
contained? or may we call it very cunning,
instead? I know now. I did not know
then, but I suspected.

' Things are not what they seem.'

CHAPTER XIV.

WHEN the summer session of the medical schools was drawing to a close, Willie got leave of absence from his hospital work, and came to visit his father.

I made an early endeavour to discover if Willie's opinion of Marshall agreed with my own.

' Willie, did I hear you say that you saw Marshall yesterday ?'

' You did. I met him as I came from the station.'

' Now, Willie, honestly, what do you think of Marshall ?'

' Jupiter ! what a question.'

16—2

'Nobody ever taught you that you mustn't say "Jupiter," I suppose?' I interrupted.

'Of course not! though perhaps——'

'Never mind; only it reminded me so of old days. You used to be so fond of appealing to Jupiter when you were a boy, and I caught it, and carried it to Dalestonbury; and how Aunt Marshall snubbed me about it! Now, if I had had the good fortune to be a male creature, I should say "Jupiter" at this moment. Oh, what privileges of sex!'

'When women get their rights, you girls will say all that we say, unreproved, I suppose? Nice times those will be!'

'The "grey pre-eminence of man" is to be assailed all round, you think? I don't know anything about it, except that I wish I had been a man. Well, return to where you left off: "Jupiter! what a question!" you said. Go on.'

'What do you want to know?'

'Your opinion of our brother Marshall. Be serious, Willie; I am in earnest.'

'But what an absurd thing to ask a fellow! I think he makes a very good priest.'

'Oh, you do? Then I think you don't know much. You must have seen him a good deal, too, in all these years. Do you think he is amiable?'

'Not by nature. On the contrary, I think he is the most morose man I ever knew. But he has good manners, don't you see; so it doesn't matter.'

'It doesn't matter to those who are not in any way dependent on him, no doubt. Now tell me, do you know his wife?'

'Yes, I know her—in a way. I saw her when they were first married; and have since, at times.'

'Do you suppose her to be a happy wife?'

'Oh, my dear Harry, I can't form opinions

on such domestic points. What are you driving at, I want to know ?'

' How long is it since you saw this young Mrs. Marshall ?'

' It must be—let's think—yes, two years. They stayed here, you know, for some little time before he was old enough to be ordained priest, and I saw her then when I came down.'

' Was Marshall kind to her then ?'

' What a cross-examination ! What does all this mean, Harry ?'

' I saw her yesterday, and she did not look happy.'

' But, my dear Harry, she never did look happy. She always looked as if she had just been weeping. Some women are like that, you know. What's that thing Toole quotes : " It is their nature *to.*" They cry for nothing or anything. Hysterical diathesis, of course. Those little fat fair women generally have more or less of it.'

' Oh, Willie, Willie !'

' What is it ?'

' You have answered my question now! Poor little creature ! And you have not seen her for the last two years ; nor has father seen her for a long time. You give her up to the tender mercies of Marshall, and let her feel that the family she has come into simply ignores and despises her.'

' Come, Harry, don't talk nonsense. Have you seen her ? Yes, you said so, I remember. Well, now, allow me to say that I think the master did almost too much in allowing her ever to come here. He had better have found another shop for Marshall, in my humble opinion. As to leaving her to her husband, why, of course. He is as cross as a bear, very likely ; but, then, some women like that way, I am told—don't respect anything else.'

' Now, Willie ! You can't believe it. Where do you get that experience from ? Does Uncle

Marshall make his wife weep every day? Does Uncle Henry snarl at his wife constantly? Those are the two households you know best.'

Willie laughed out at this, in his merry way.

'Fancy Uncle Henry snarling at a lady! And fancy Aunt Marshall crying because her husband forgot to call her by a tender name! But, then, see how different the women are from one another! Depend upon it, Harry, a wife generally makes her husband whatever he is.'

'Perhaps so, when the man is of a refined nature, or when the woman is of a strong one; but with many exceptions to your theory in practice. Like a slave-owner with a slave——'

'Oh, Harry, you just now told me that you knew nothing about women's rights, and there is the very tone of it! Comparing

matrimony to slavery. " The wife is a slave."
That is the very thing to say, and I declare
you said it in the very manner.'

'I did not say that.'

But he took himself out of the room, pre-
tending not to hear my protest. I remained,
feeling more pitifully than before, even,
towards the poor young wife whose sorrows
I had divined in a moment, though men so
tender-hearted towards women as my father
and Willie had been quite unable to believe in
them.

'One would suppose,' I soliloquised, 'that
men think that so long as a wife is not
starved or kicked by her husband, she cannot
have anything to complain of with regard to
him. I suspect that men do not understand
how cruelly a woman can feel such seclusion
and isolation as this poor Fanny is living in,
and such brutality as I saw her husband display towards her the other day. Men have

so many interests outside their homes ; they could not be made utterly miserable by their domesticity, I suppose, and so they cannot imagine how its storms can shake a woman. But I could see at once how that poor little creature is tormented day by day. Then my father and Willie do not see her. I wish I could help her! Very likely when I come to stay at home I shall be able. I would like to deliver any living thing from Marshall's clutches !'

During the rest of my stay at the Castle, I saw my sister-in-law twice only, and each time in her husband's presence. I called upon her once or twice, alone, but received an excuse from the servant on each occasion : 'Mrs. Abbott had an headache, and was lying down,' or ' Mrs. Abbott was very busy, and would I wait for the master?' I did not resent this, because I suspected that she was forbidden to see me alone. But the consequence was that I was almost as much a stranger to her when I left home as I had been before I arrived. Not quite so, however.

When I went, Willie accompanied me, and escorted me to the other end of England, to our Aunt Marshall's. It had been arranged that I should spend the last fortnight of the holidays there, and that Helen should be invited also. Willie seldom visited at Dalestonbury, but as he had accompanied me he remained a week there.

To my equal surprise and regret, Willie and Helen managed to get up a state of warfare between them in that week. Not, of course, actual belligerency, and open rudeness, but a constant current of antagonism and sarcasm ran between them. It was Helen's fault. Willie was much too amiable for this to be congenial to him; but Helen amused herself by annoying him, and stinging him into repartee. I was the only witness of these petty encounters of wits; in the presence of my aunt, nothing could have been more proper than Helen's maidenly reserve and quiet distance of manner.

The week soon passed over, and I was almost glad when Willie went; for I had daily feared lest his sweetness of temper should give way, and lest they might quarrel in earnest. This would have been exceedingly annoying to me, inasmuch as Willie would be at home in the house where Helen and I were to go for our first London season. I said this to Helen when Willie was gone.

' I am actually glad to get him away, you bad girl! How dared you tease him so? And how do you think he will like the prospect of having you in the same house with him in London ?'

' He will forget all about it before then,'

replied Helen, in her most contemptuous manner, as though she were sublimely indifferent to his opinions and wishes.

' Indeed he will not,' I said, 'at all events, he is certain not to forget it, even if he forgives it.'

' Ah !' said Helen, and nothing more.

It did not occur to me just then that to be remembered was exactly what she had designed. Willie might readily have forgotten her politeness in the six months that were to intervene before we went to London for our season ; he would not forget her cutting ridicule. Was it that Helen foresaw this ? She was a born diplomatist, as the future showed.

END OF VOL. I.

BILLING AND SONS, PRINTERS, GUILDFORD, SURREY.

31, SOUTHAMPTON STREET,

STRAND,

February, 1880.

NOTICE: TO AUTHORS, &c.

MESSRS. SAMUEL TINSLEY & CO. beg to intimate that they are now prepared to undertake the Publication of all classes of Books, Pamphlets, etc., etc., and will give most prompt and careful attention to any works forwarded for inspection to the above address. Messrs. S. TINSLEY & CO. have during the last few years issued a larger number of Works of Fiction, Poetry, Travel, etc., than have been published by any other firm, and have the greatest possible facilities for the speedy and satisfactory production of books of every description.

The fullest particulars will be given upon application, and every work will be carefully considered upon its own merits without any delay whatever.

Lists of Publications, etc., will be forwarded, free by post, upon application.

N.B.—Correspondents will please address carefully, as above, Messrs. SAMUEL TINSLEY & CO. *being totally distinct from any other firm.*

31, SOUTHAMPTON STREET, STRAND, *February* 20, 1880.

SAMUEL TINSLEY & CO.'S NEW PUBLICATIONS.

THE NEWEST NOVELS.
EACH IN THREE VOLUMES.

NOTICE.—New novel by the Popular Author of ' Love's Conflict,' ' Woman Against Woman,' ' Petronel,' etc.

THE ROOT OF ALL EVIL. By FLORENCE MARRYAT, Author of ' Love's Conflict,' ' Woman Against Woman,' etc. 3 vols., 31s. 6d. The *Morning Post* says :—' It can be honestly recommended to those who enjoy a good strong story, capitally written, in this clever writer's best style.'

Hacklander's Europäisches Sclavenleben.
EUROPEAN SLAVE LIFE. By F. W. HACKLANDER. Translated by E. WOLTMANN. 3 vols., 31s. 6d. The *Athenæum* says :—' Dickens could never have written or inspired Hacklander's most famous story. . . . The English rendering is excellent, reading like an original rather than a translation, and should secure for the novel a considerable English circulation.'

LOVE'S BONDAGE. By LAURENCE BROOKE, Author of ' The Queen of Two Worlds.' 3 vols.. 31s. 6d. The *Athenæum* says :—' " Love's Bondage " is worth reading.'

THE OLD LOVE IS THE NEW. By MAURICE WILTON. 3 vols., 31s. 6d.

IN SHEEP'S CLOTHING. By Mrs. HARRY BENNETT EDWARDS, Author of ' A Tantalus Cup.' 3 vols., 31s. 6d. The *Scotsman* says :—' There is unquestionable power in Mrs. Bennett Edwards's novel, " In Sheep's Clothing "—power both of conception and of execution.'

FISHING IN DEEP WATERS. By RICHARD ROWLATT. 3 vols., 31s. 6d.

DRIFTED TOGETHER. By ELIZABETH SAVILE. 3 vols., 31s. 6d.

EACH COMPLETE IN ONE VOLUME.

NOTICE.—A Third Edition of this important work, with new preface, is now ready.

DON GARCIA IN ENGLAND. Scenes and Characters from English Life. By GEORGE WINDLE SANDYS. 8vo., handsomely bound, 12s.

A YEAR IN INDIA. By ANTHONY GEORGE SHIELL. 1 vol., demy 8vo., 14s.

SQUATTERMANIA ; or, Phases of Antipodean Life. By ERRO. Crown 8vo., 7s. 6d.

THE VIKING. By M. R. Crown 8vo., 7s. 6d.

WHO WAS SHE ? By EFFIE A. CLARKE. Crown 8vo., 7s. 6d.

THE LITTLE PRINCESS COLOMBE. By GINA ROSE, Author of ' Sorrentina.' Crown 8vo., 7s. 6d.

THE LAST OF THE KERDRECS. By WILLIAM MINTERN, Author of ' Travels West.' Crown 8vo., 7s. 6d.

A GREAT LADY. From the German of DEWALL. Translated by LOUISE HARRISON. Crown 8vo., 7s. 6d.

THE HEIRESS, NOT THE WOMAN. By ALAN GRANT. Crown 8vo., 7s. 6d.

London : Samuel Tinsley & Co., 31, Southampton St., Strand.

BOOKS FOR THE YOUNG.

UNCLE GRUMPY.
And other PLAYS for CHILDREN.
By R. ST. JOHN CORBET.

Crown 8vo., 3s.

A Collection of short, original, easily learned, easily acted, easily mounted Pieces for Private Representation by Boys and Girls.

STORIES FOR MAMMA'S DARLINGS.
Ten Stories for Children.
By AMANDA MATORKA BLANKENSTEIN.

Crown 8vo., 3s. 6d.

The *Brighton Examiner* says :—'This is an excellent story book, adapted for young children.'
The *Dundee Advertiser* says :—' These stories are excellent in their moral tone.'
The *Sunderland Herald* says :—' It is an excellent gift-book.'
Lloyd's News says :—' These stories for children are excellent.'

A SPLENDID STORY FOR BOYS.

FRANK BLAKE, THE TRAPPER.
By MRS. HARDY,
AUTHOR OF 'THE CASTAWAY'S HOME,' 'UP NORTH,' ETC.

Handsomely bound and illustrated, 5s.

The *Times* says:—' " Frank Blake " is a story in which bears, Indians, comical negroes, and the various other *dramatis personæ* of such works play their parts with capital effect. This is a tale of the good old-fashioned sort.'
The *Pall Mall Gazette* says :—' " Frank Blake " abounds in adventures of a familiar and popular kind.'
The *Saturday Review* says :—' " Frank Blake " is the book wherewith to spend a happy day at the romantic and tender age of thirteen. It scarcely yields in interest to the " Rifle-Rangers," or " The White Chief."'
The *Guardian* says :—' It is a book of unusual power of its kind.'
The *Scotsman* says :—' Mrs. Hardy has written, in " Frank Blake, the Trapper," a book absolutely crowded with stirring adventure.'
The *Manchester Guardian* says :—' " Frank Blake " is a thoroughly fresh, healthy, and interesting account of a boy's adventures in the Far West.'
The *Leeds Mercury* says:—'In " Frank Blake " there are many humorous passages and a finely sustained narrative.'
The *Shrewsbury Chronicle* says :—' We doubt if any one, even Capt. Mayne Reid, would have surrounded Frank Blake's life with more interesting incidents than this accomplished authoress has done.'
The *Birmingham Daily Gazette* says :—' By means of a capital story a good deal of information is incidently furnished ; and the lad who is not charmed with the tale will indeed be difficult to please.'
The *Preston Herald* says :—' We can strongly recommend it to those parents who desire to place in the hands of their sons and nephews a present of sterling merit.

LONDON :

Samuel Tinsley & Co., 31, Southampton Street, Strand.

IN THE PRESS.

Important New Work by CAPTAIN CREAGH.

ARMENIANS, KOORDS, AND TURKS; or, The Past,
Present, and Future of Armenia. By JAMES CREAGH, Author of
'Over the Borders of Christendom and Eslamiah.' 2 vols., large post
8vo., 24s.

JACK ALLYN'S FRIENDS. By G. WEBB APPLETON,
Author of 'Catching a Tartar,' and 'Frozen Hearts.' 3 vols., 31s. 6d.

HOLLYWOOD. By ANNIE L. WALKER, Author of 'A
Canadian Heroine,' 'Against Her Will,' etc. 3 vols., 31s. 6d.

CARMELA. By the Princess OLGA CANTACUZENE, Author
of 'In the Spring of My Life.' Translated by EUGENIA KLAUS, with
the Author's approval. 3 vols., 31s. 6d.

THE BURTONS OF DUNROE. By M. W. BREW. 3 vols.,
31s. 6d.

FROZEN, BUT NOT DEAD. A Novel. By A. B. WOODWARD.
Crown 8vo., 7s. 6d.

EVELINE; or, The Mysteries. A Tale of Ancient Britain.
By M. DE VERE SMITH. Crown 8vo., 7s. 6d.

CLAUDE BRANCA'S PROMISE. By ALICE CLIFTON. 3
vols., 31s. 6d.

HARRINGTON'S FORTUNES. By ALFRED RANDALL.
3 vols., 31s. 6d.

Author's Note.—The main incidents of this story comprise events caused
by insurrectionary movements agitating Ireland during the year 1848, and
have a peculiar interest for Liberals, Conservatives, and all law-abiding
citizens at the present time.

KINGS IN EXILE. By ALPHONSE DAUDET. From the
French, by express authority of the Author. 3 vols., 31s. 6d.

LORD GARLFORD'S FREAK. By JAMES B. BAYNARD,
Author of 'The Rector of Oxbury.' 3 vols., 31s. 6d.

A FEARFUL ADVERSARY. By P. JILLARD. 3 vols.,
31s. 6d.

SOUTH AFRICAN WAR VERSES. Dedicated to the
Defenders of Rorke's Drift. By FREDERIC ATKINSON, M.A., Trin. Coll.,
Cambridge. In wrapper, 1s.

THE BATTLE OF SENLAC, and other Poems. By the
Rev. J. M. ASHLEY, B.C.L. Crown 8vo., 5s.

LONDON :

Samuel Tinsley & Co., 31, Southampton Street, Strand.

/